THE MYSTERY OF AN OLD MURDER

LAURA BRETT

The Mystery Of An Old Murder

DEDICATION

To Martin, without whom all this would not have been possible. I love you, my darling!

The Mystery Of An Old Murder

CONTENTS

The Mystery Of An Old Murder

ACKNOWLEDGMENTS

Writing a novel is a lonely affair, yet there are some people I do need to thank for both their support and their wealth of wisdom. Sharon, Leslie and Belinda, thank you for always being there. Mrs. Benton, you are an authority on all things old but not forgotten! Mr. Lawrence, fountain of youth, my gratitude goes out to you for hours and hours of research. Last but not least, Martin. Thank you honey for being there on good days, on bad days, and all moments in between!

The Mystery Of An Old Murder

CHAPTER 1

UNEXPECTED VISITORS

The railway passes close to Saltleigh now; you can see the tall church tower and the gabled rectory as the train enters the little wayside station, where flowers bloom all the year round in the soft Cornish air. But railroads had not been heard of when Marjorie Drew was a girl; Plymouth and Bodmin were then farther off from Saltleigh than London is now, and in all her life of seventeen years Marjorie had seen no town larger than Driscombe, the tiny market town four miles off, through which the mail-coach passed twice a day, waking the echoes of its paved street with clattering wheels and bugle blast, and bringing with it for a few moments the bustle and excitement of the great world beyond the hills.

It was the coach which brought the London Gazette for the rector of Saltleigh, Marjorie's father, that precious sheet with its scanty war-news and lists of dead and wounded, so eagerly watched for by those who had dear ones fighting.

War had been a familiar word to Marjorie from babyhood. She had been in the little gray marketplace of Driscombe one day in early November when the coach came in, all decked with flags and flowers, but with crape twined among the flowers, bringing the news of Trafalgar and the death of Nelson. She was only eight years old, but her little heart swelled with pride and grief just as did the hearts of the grown-up men and women about her. Those were days when there was terror in the very name of Bonaparte; when the fear of invasion was heavy on England; and Marjorie, child as she was, understood what the victory meant, and what England owed to the hero who was gone.

The fear of invasion passed, but the war went on, and its shadow fell more darkly on the quiet Rectory as Marjorie grew older. Her brothers were now away, fighting for their country. And into her mother's eyes had come that far-off, patient, waiting look that mothers' eyes wore in those days. But it was not all shadow; there were days of pride and rejoicing, when even Mrs. Drew could smile and be as hopeful as Marjorie. Letters had come from Jack's colonel, and from the captain of Ned's ship, praising the boys; and one never-to-be-forgotten day Jack's name was in the Gazette, not in those dreadful lists, scanned with sickening dread by so many loving eyes, but in despatches, mentioned for gallant conduct at Badajoz. Mrs. Drew went about the house that day with her delicate head held high, and Marjorie saddled her white pony and rode across to tell Aunt Eleanor, who was staying at Westmead for a week; and when she came back, the villagers had set the bells ringing in the old tower, and the valley was jubilant with the sound of the merry chimes.

But dearer than anything were the letters from the boys themselves; letters only to be looked for at uncertain intervals, and to be read again and again, till the edges of the broad sheets wore away.

Marjorie had one of these precious sheets in her wallet as she rode home from Driscombe on her white pony one February afternoon. February though it was, there were few signs of winter in the narrow sheltered lanes through which she rode. The grassy banks were brightly green, and starred with celandines and daisies; the blackthorn was in bloom, and so was the gorse; and once Marjorie had got of her pony to pick some primroses which she had espied in a sheltered spot. The sky overhead was softly blue, and though the morning had brought with it a slight touch of frost, the air now was like the breath of April. No wonder the birds were singing, calling to each other in clear, soft notes from hedgerow to hedgerow, as if spring were already come.

Marjorie began to sing herself as she cantered on, to sing like the birds in very happiness of heart; the winter was over and gone, the long warm days of summer were at hand.

The district was a thinly populated one, and she met no one on the road. But as she approached the crossroads, about half-way between Saltleigh and Driscombe, she saw a post-chaise standing there. The post-boy had got down and was trying to decipher the names on the dilapidated finger-post, while one of the occupants of the chaise, a ruddy-faced old gentleman with very white hair and whiskers, was leaning out, pointing with his stick and talking in a loud impatient voice.

He turned round on hearing the sound of the pony's hoofs.

"Here is somebody at last!" he exclaimed. And then added, staring through his gold-rimmed spectacles at Marjorie, "Why, bless my soul, you must be Marjorie Drew! Don't tell me you are not, for I won't believe it."

The Mystery Of An Old Murder

Marjorie was slightly taken aback at this abrupt address from a perfect stranger, but before she could answer, one of the ladies in the chaise, a round-faced, bright-eyed little woman, bent forward to speak.

"We are trying to find our way to Saltleigh Rectory, my dear. You must be Marjorie Drew, I am sure. You are so like your Aunt Nell."

Marjorie flushed up with pleasure. She loved to be told she was like her dear Aunt Nell. "I wondered how you knew me," she said shyly.

"But you don't know us, eh?" demanded the white-haired old gentleman.

"No, sir," said Marjorie, smiling as she met his eyes, gleaming kindly under his bushy white eyebrows. He had taken off his spectacles, and was rubbing them with his yellow silk handkerchief, and he looked much less alarming without them.

"But you have heard your father speak of Roger Bulteel? That is my name, little girl."

His wife again interposed.

"Your mother must forgive us for taking her by surprise like this, but we could not pass within a dozen miles of Saltleigh and not stop. We have been to Plymouth to meet my niece Kitty, who has come from

London to spend the summer with us. Kitty's brother is in your Jack's regiment, my dear. Has he mentioned Captain Hollis in his letters?"

"Often, madam," Marjorie answered, looking with smiling eagerness at the young lady in a very fine pelisse, who sat opposite Mr. and Mrs. Bulteel, with her hands hidden in an enormous muff. She had a small, rather pretty face, but it was thin and pinched, and the smile and bow she gave Marjorie had something curiously affected and un-youthful about them. Marjorie felt sorry for her as she looked at her sallow cheeks. She thought she must be ill.

"Kitty is very tired," Mrs. Bulteel said. "Are we far from the Rectory now, my dear?"

"It is just over the hill," answered Marjorie in her bright voice. "I will ride on to tell mother you are coming. How glad she and father and Aunt Nell will be! You cannot

miss the road now. It is straight up the hill."

"I knew it!" exclaimed Mr. Bulteel with a triumphant glance at his wife. "Didn't I tell you so, Mary? But what do you mean by having a finger-post like that at your crossroads, Miss Marjorie? We were glad enough to hear your pony's hoofs, I can tell you. Kitty here thought we were lost for good, got into a kind of No Man's Land. You wished yourself back in Lunnon town—eh, Kit? But you ride on, my dear, and show us the way. Though I was certain the hill was our road."

Marjorie cantered off, and Mr. Bulteel bent out of the chaise to look after her with an approving glance. "I knew who she was the moment I set eyes on her," he said to his wife. "She's just what Nell was at her age, isn't she? Just such another happy, bright-eyed creature, full of fun and laughter. Well, well, it is a hard world for some of us."

A spark of curiosity showed in Kitty's round eyes. "Miss Lane was engaged once to that Mr. Carew you and uncle were speaking of yesterday, was she not?" she said to her aunt "I heard mother talking to Lady Tremayne about it at one of our card-parties."

"What business had you to be there, pray?" demanded her uncle. "Little girls should be in bed and asleep before card-parties begin. And don't you mention the name of Carew here. An old story like that is best forgotten."

"I never repeat things," said Miss Kitty with a little toss of her head. "And I am not a little girl, Uncle James. I am sixteen."

Mr. Bulteel looked at her with twinkling eyes.

"That's a great age indeed, Kit. But you'll be younger in a few years. Won't she, Aunt Mary?"

"Your uncle is fond of teasing, my dear," Mrs. Bulteel said smilingly. "You must not mind it."

But Kitty's face did not lose its expression of offended dignity. She disliked extremely to be called Kit; Kitty was quite bad enough. She had tried in vain to make her mother and brother call her Catharina. But—Kit! She could not forgive her uncle for addressing her, a London young lady of fashion, by such a ridiculous title. She had expected to be treated very differently indeed.

Mrs. Bulteel understood far better than her husband how Kitty's feelings had been hurt, and hastened to say something pleasant.

"We hope Mrs. Drew will allow Marjorie to spend some weeks with us soon, Kitty. You will like to have a companion of your own age. We want you to have a happy summer."

Kitty looked a little brighter at this. She felt that it would be amusing to have a little country girl like Marjorie to talk to, and dazzle with her descriptions of London gaieties.

"I should think they would be glad to let her

come, Aunt Mary," she said. "It would be a change for her. How dull it must be to live in the depths of the country like this! I should die of the dumps."

"Marjorie didn't look dull, my dear," said her aunt. "The country has its pleasures as well as London, you know. But look, isn't that a pretty scene?"

They had reached the brow of the hill, and the green valley lay below them with its trees and its winding stream. The church and the village were close together, and a long wooded meadow divided them from the gabled rectory, which was near the foot of the hill, surrounded by a large carefully-kept garden sloping on one side down to the stream.

It was a low, irregularly-built house, with diamond-paned windows, and a wide hospitable porch, thickly overgrown with creepers. The garden beds were brilliant with crocuses, violet and yellow, and the gravel-path up to the house was edged on each side by snowdrops, and red daisies, and early wallflowers.

There was no carriage-drive, as Kitty's eyes were quick to note. The chaise stopped at the gate, but before it stopped the tall rector came hurrying from the house, and he was at the gate to meet them.

It was a warm welcome he gave to the travellers; he, as well as his wife and sister-in-law, had been born and bred in St. Mawan, and, though for years he had not been near the place, he cherished a warm affection for it still.

"Come in, come in," he cried ; "Thomas will look after the chaise. He will be here in a moment. Start again in an hour? Nonsense, old friends. Hear what my wife and Nell have to say to that! Nell will be here presently, Marjorie has gone to meet her. Here they are, Edith. They talk of starting again this evening. But that's not to be allowed, is it, my dear?"

He had brought them into the porch, and Kitty saw a tall, slender, elegant-looking woman, with dark hair turning slightly gray, and quick-glancing hazel eyes, who came running forward to meet them with outstretched hands. Kitty could not help confessing to herself that a country welcome was a very pleasant thing to receive, and that Mrs. Drew, except that her cap was not of the latest fashion, did not look at all like a country parson's wife.

She was very glad when it was settled they should stay at the Rectory that night, instead of going on in that jolting post-chaise to St. Mawan. The long drive from Plymouth had made her feel miserably tired. It was pleasant to be taken up to a pretty room looking into the garden, and to be tucked up on a sofa at the window by Mrs. Drew's gentle hands.

The Mystery Of An Old Murder

"Marjorie shall come and fetch you when it is tea-time," were almost the last words Kitty heard. Before Mrs. Drew and her aunt left the room she was asleep.

"She has been ill," Mrs. Bulteel said, as she looked down for a moment at the pale little face of the sleeper. "I hope the summer will do her good. Would you let Marjorie stay with us for a time, Edith? You promised last year that we should have her someday."

"She would like to go," said Mrs. Drew with a faint sigh, a sigh Mrs. Bulteel understood; "she questions us eagerly about St. Mawan. It does not seem right that neither she nor the boys have ever been there. But John thought it best."

"But surely now, after so many years," began Mrs. Bulteel, and then checked herself and did not speak again till they had crossed the broad landing and reached the top of the stairs. The front-door stood wide open, and from where they stood they could see the gravel walk in front of the porch. Marjorie was standing there talking to Mr. Bulteel, and by her side was a tall woman in black, with a print sun-bonnet over her fair hair. Mrs. Bulteel gave a great start as her eyes fell on her. She laid her hand on Mrs. Drew's arm.

"Is that Nell?" she said in a low voice. "Oh, Edith, how changed she is!"

"Could you expect her not to be changed?" said Mrs. Drew with a tremor in her voice. "But she is well and strong, thank God. She is our guardian angel, Lucy. That is what John calls her. And he knows better than anyone what she has been to us and to the parish. Her life is an utterly unselfish one. And she says she is happy."

Mrs. Drew sighed again as she stopped speaking, and Mrs. Bulteel glanced at her. "Edith, do you think she has forgotten?" she asked.

Mrs. Drew shrank back as if the question had touched some open wound. But she answered quickly. "We never speak of it," she said. "It is years since she has mentioned Robert's name to me. But she has not forgotten, Lucy. John thinks she has, because she is so cheerful always, so interested in other people's affairs. But I know her better than John." She paused a moment, and then added in a lower voice, as if afraid the group standing outside the porch might hear, "He is away still, is he not? The Manor House is shut up?"

"Yes, he is in London. James hears from him, but not often. He never speaks of himself, but I am afraid his life is a very lonely one. I wish he would come home." She paused, but Mrs. Drew did not speak, and she went on more quickly : "Edith, has Marjorie been told? Kitty seems to have heard something in London;

she was asking us questions just now."

Mrs. Drew's delicate eyebrows drew together in a little pained frown. "Do people gossip about it still?" she said. "I hoped it was all forgotten by strangers after so many years. No, Marjorie knows nothing; we thought it better to keep it from her. She is such a child still. But you say Kitty is only two months older. I can hardly believe it. She looks two years older."

"How delighted she would be to hear you say so!" said Mrs. Bulteel, with a laugh. She was glad to escape from the painful subject they had been talking of. "Kitty wants to be grown-up. Her little head has been turned by her mother's fashionable friends. But she is a good girl at heart; she won't hurt your Marjorie."

"I am not afraid," said the mother, with a proud little smile. "But you must speak to John, Lucy. And now, let us go down; Nell will be anxious to see you."

CHAPTER 2

AUNT NELL

Marjorie was just two years old when her grandmother and Aunt Nell came to Saltleigh.

They lived in a house of their own till Mrs. Lane died, but then the house was given up, and Marjorie could hardly remember a time when her darling Aunt Nell did not live with them.

She knew nothing of her aunt's brief engagement to Robert Carew, or of the tragic circumstances that had ended it; so that she did not guess why her mother had sent her to meet Aunt Nell to prepare her for the visitors from St. Mawan.

She ran gleefully along the meadow path, and in a few moments saw her aunt emerge from the grove of trees that hid the village. A couple of rosy-cheeked children were running at her side, and she was talking gaily to them, but on seeing Marjorie she sent them back, and came on alone with a quickened step.

"Marjorie, you have some news—you have a letter from the boys!" she exclaimed, as she drew near to speak.

"Aunt Nell, you are a witch! Yes, there is a letter from Ned; such a long letter, mother has not read it yet. But there is more news. We have visitors—visitors who came in a post-chaise with yellow wheels. Guess who? From St. Mawan!"

A quiver went over Miss Lane's delicate features. Her eyes met Marjorie's in a swift, startled glance the girl could not understand.

"From St. Mawan!" she faltered.

"Did I say from St. Mawan? The post-chaise came from Plymouth; but the visitors belong to St. Mawan—at least two of them do. The third is a fine young lady from London, who despises poor country folk. Oh, Aunt Nell, how puzzled you look! Think of a very fierce-looking old gentleman, with a very red face and very white hair, and gold-rimmed spectacles. Can't you guess now ? And his wife is a dear old motherly body. I fell in love with her at first sight. And when she smiles she puckers up her eyebrows like this."

"Oh, Marjorie, you mimic; of course I guess now," laughed Miss Lane. "It is Mr. and Mrs. Bulteel. But you said his hair was white. Is it white? It used to be raven black when I knew him;" and she ended her laughing speech with a sigh Marjorie did not catch.

"It is white now. He must have looked fiercer still when his hair was black. But he has kind eyes. I am not very much afraid of him."

"He is one of the kindest men in the world," declared Miss Lane warmly. "It is only at first people are afraid of him. They soon find out how good he is, and some of them take advantage of it. He would have been a much richer man if he had not been so good-natured."

"He has a bank, hasn't he?" asked Marjorie. "I have heard father speaking of it—Bulteel's Bank."

Miss Lane looked at her with a smile.

"Bulteel's Bank is one of the institutions of St. Mawan, Marjorie. The family have been bankers there for nearly two hundred years. I really believe the people think its notes safer than the Bank of England's."

"Dear me, no wonder he looks so fierce and authoritative! I shall begin to be afraid of him again. But, Aunt Nell, just think, he knew me in a moment.

How was that, I wonder? He had never set eyes on me before. They were pulled up at the crossroads, and the post-boy was trying to read that poor old finger-post, while Mr. Bulteel waved his stick and shouted at him. It was a mercy I came up to them. They would be there now, I believe. And when he turned round and saw me, he called out in an instant, 'You are Marjorie Drew. Don't tell me you are not, for I won't believe you.'"

She said it, drawing down her eyebrows and thrusting out her lower lip exactly as Mr. Bulteel had done. From childhood Marjorie had had wonderful powers of observation and mimicry. But for her generous, healthy impulses, the gift of mimicry might have been a dangerous one, but she had never been known to use it unkindly. And her father had often said that he would rather trust to Marjorie's judgment of a person than to that of many older people.

"Marjorie, how do you do it?" laughed her aunt. "You could only have seen him for a moment. You have wonderful eyes, dear child."

Marjorie softly shook the arm she held. "But how did Mr. Bulteel know me, Aunt Nell? He had never seen me before. How did he know me?"

Marjorie asked the question in a tone of gleeful triumph. And it was her tone and the merry glance which accompanied it that interpreted her meaning to Miss Lane. She shook her head with a smile that was more than half sad.

"I was only a year or two older than you are now, Marjorie, when Mr. Bulteel saw me last. He would not say we were alike now, dear. He will find it hard to remember me."

"Aunt Nell, you shall not talk like that, as if you were an old woman! If you have altered, it is only to be prettier and sweeter and dearer than ever," cried Marjorie fondly. "But there are father and Mr. Bulteel waiting for us at the gate. Am I walking too fast, Aunt Nell? You look so pale. I wish you would let me go and read to Nancy tomorrow. Her room is always so hot, it tires you out."

"Yes, I am very tired," Miss Lane said. She had felt herself begin to tremble in every limb as she caught sight of Mr. Bulteel at the gate. It was so many years since she had seen anyone from St. Mawan. "But let us hasten on, dear. They are coming to meet us."

Miss Lane had been right in thinking that Mr. Bulteel would find her changed. He found it difficult at first to realize that she was indeed that merry, light-hearted girl he had known fourteen years before. The bloom of youth had gone from her face, the sparkle from her eyes; she looked years older than Marjorie's mother. But as they walked back to the house and stood talking before the porch in the soft evening light, he saw how beautiful she was still, more beautiful than she had ever been. Her face had gained far more than it had lost; it had a charm beyond all mere youthful prettiness. And though there were depths in her eyes a smile never reached, it was not a sad face; a ready, cheerful sympathy spoke in every look. He understood what Mrs. Drew had meant by calling her their guardian angel. It was plain that the rector and Marjorie were devoted to her. Whenever she spoke they turned to listen, as if her lightest word were too precious to be lost.

When Mrs. Drew and Mrs. Bulteel came downstairs, Marjorie slipped away, in obedience to a whispered word from her mother.

She went to her room and changed her dress, and then stole softly into her mother's room, where Kitty still lay asleep on the big sofa.

Kitty opened her eyes presently, and after gazing round her in a bewildered way for a moment or two, lifted herself on her elbow to get a better view of Marjorie, who was curled up on the broad cushioned window-seat with a book in her hand.

"I am awake," she said after a moment, in a slightly plaintive voice. She thought Marjorie ought not to have been so absorbed in her book as to be unaware that her nap was over.

Marjorie jumped lightly up and came towards her. "Are you rested?" she said cheerfully. "Tea will be ready soon."

Kitty lay looking at her for a moment without replying. She had no fault to find with Marjorie's white dress, scanty in the skirt and very short in the waist, with its frills of dainty lace round neck and sleeves. And her coral necklace was almost as good as Kitty's own. But her fair curly hair was arranged in quite a childish fashion, and Kitty reflected with much complacency on the high comb her mother had given her for a Christmas present, and which she meant to wear that evening.

"I must have been asleep nearly an hour," she said, after her deliberate survey of Marjorie from head to foot. "It is getting dark, isn't it? How could you see to read by this light? Madame Le Clair would never let me read in a bad light; it hurts the eyes. She was my governess. She was really the Marquise Le Clair; her husband was guillotined by those dreadful French people who killed the king and Marie Antoinette. They took away all her estates, and she has to teach for a living. It was a great advantage for me to be taught by her. But I have no governess now, my education is finished. I suppose you have lessons still. Do you go to school, or have you a governess?"

"I have two, mother and Aunt Nell," said Marjorie smiling. She was very much relieved to find that Kitty was ready to talk. She had feared that conversation would be difficult. "And father teaches me a little too. But tell me about your French governess, Madame la Marquise. Poor woman, how sad for her to lose everything!"

"Oh, she was very cheerful! And you would never have guessed that she was noble. She looked just a brown-faced, shabby old woman. And, good gracious, how strict she was! She would make me enter the room ten times over till I made my curtsy in a proper manner. I will give you some lessons if you like."

Marjorie was secretly amused at this offer to teach her deportment. If Kitty knew how to curtsy she did not know how to walk. Her short, mincing steps made Marjorie feel inclined to shake her.

They were now in the little guest-room, which had been prepared for Kitty. Marjorie was helping her to unpack the small box that had been carried upstairs from the chaise. Kitty explained that most of her dresses had gone on in her big box by the carrier, and would reach St. Mawan some time that week.

"But I have scarcely any new things," she said somewhat discontentedly; "mother said I should not want them down here. But I have a book of fashions I can show you. And I will give you the pattern of my new black silk spencer. It only came home last week. You could send the pattern to your dressmaker and have one made exactly like it. You will come to St. Mawan soon, will you not? And then you shall see all my things."

Marjorie's eyes opened wide. "But I am not going to St. Mawan," she said.

Kitty turned from the glass where she was fastening up her hair and tapped her gaily on the cheek. She had to stand on her tiptoes to do it, for Marjorie was nearly a head taller. "My dear creature, you must come; Aunt Mary is determined to have you. And I am sure we should agree. You are a dear little soul. Positively you must come."

Despite Kitty's affectations there was real good-nature in her sallow little face, and Marjorie's heart grew warm towards her. "I must hear what mother says about it," she said. "I should like to go. I have never been to St. Mawan, though mother and father and Aunt Nell were all born there."

"It must be a dull little place," said Kitty, shrugging her shoulders, a gesture she had caught from her marquise. "You ought to come to London, you dear little country mouse. I shall make mother invite you when I go back. But now we must have you at St. Mawan. Your cousin Carew does not live there now, so that there is no reason why you should not come."

Kitty had said the last words without thinking, but she recollected her promise to her aunt as she saw Marjorie's bewildered look. She turned away biting her lips, pretending to be busy with her comb. But she could not help being amused and gratified at discovering that she knew more than Marjorie about her family history. It added to the feelings of superiority Marjorie's country breeding and evident simplicity had already aroused in her.

"Do you like this comb?" she asked, as she put a last touch or two to her clustered curls. "One like it would suit you, I am sure. But your dress is pretty. It is real Indian muslin, isn't it?"

"Yes, Uncle George sent it to me from India. Kitty, I did not understand you just now. Were you speaking of Mr. Robert Carew? He—"

"Don't ask me any questions, my dear girl. I ought to have been quite silent. And I meant nothing, nothing. Is it time for us to go downstairs now? I am quite ready."

Kitty had expected to find Marjorie bent on cross-examining her, and was surprised and not a little disappointed to find that she dropped the subject at once. There is not much gratification to be gained from refusing to disclose a secret if your companion takes you at your word at once, and shows no further curiosity about it.

But Marjorie, though too proud and too loyal to seek to learn from Kitty what her parents and Aunt Nell had not told her, could not forget Kitty's words; she tried hard to dismiss them from her mind, but they obstinately lingered there. It hurt her a little to find out that Kitty knew something about St. Mawan history which she had not been allowed to know. And she wondered if she would be told before going to St. Mawan. For it was settled that her father should take her there early in March. Mr. Drew would only be able to stay for a day or two, but Marjorie was to stay a month or more.

CHAPTER 3

A TRAGIC HISTORY

Marjorie had never been away from home before, and this visit to St. Mawan was looked on as an important event, not only by herself, but by all the household. The set of shirts for Ned, the sailor, over which so many winter hours had been spent, was put aside, and much anxious consultation went on in reference to Marjorie's wardrobe. Mrs. Drew and Aunt Nell did not intend their girl to be altogether outshone by London Kitty. And simple as her new dresses were, the materials were of the finest, and the lace on them might have been worn by a princess. Then there was a new brown pelisse trimmed with sable, and a straw bonnet with ostrich feathers that made Marjorie feel like a grown-up young lady. She had an honest delight in her new clothes, and but for the haunting memory of Kitty's words would have looked forward with unmixed pleasure to her visit.

Once or twice she had felt tempted to repeat to her mother and Aunt Nell what Kitty had said, but each time she was held back by the fear lest by doing so she should force them to tell her what they did not wish her to know. And the end of February approached, and the time for her visit drew near without her mentioning the subject. But little as she suspected it, her mother and Miss Lane were already aware of what Kitty had said to her. Kitty had confessed her indiscretion to her aunt, who had told Mrs. Drew. And before the visitors left the Rectory, it was decided that Marjorie should hear the whole sad story before going to St. Mawan. Aunt Nell took upon herself the task of telling her, and had tried more than once to begin. But she found it very difficult to speak of those dark days of her youth, in whose shadow she was living still. Yet she would not let Mrs. Drew tell Marjorie; she had always meant, she said, to tell Marjorie herself. And she was glad the time had come when she might do so.

Two days before the time fixed for Marjorie's leaving home, her father and mother went to dine at Westmead, a pretty house on the other side of the valley, occupied by Mr. Drew's cousin. Aunt Nell had been invited, but had declined to go. By remaining at home she would have a long quiet evening with Marjorie, which was what she wanted.

The Mystery Of An Old Murder

It was Tuesday afternoon, and Marjorie rode in to Driscombe as usual for the letters. The mail was disappointing, for there were only business letters for her father. But there was a letter with an American post-mark for old Nancy White, which Marjorie felt sure must be from her son. She knew Nancy would not get it till market-day unless she carried it to her, as the old woman never came into the town except to sell her eggs and fowls at the weekly market. It was a long way round to her cottage, which was a solitary dwelling on Driscombe Common, but Marjorie could not leave the letter lying in the post-mistress's box when the sight of it would be so precious to the lonely mother.

She rode fast, but it was almost dark when she got home. Thomas took her pony, and she walked quickly up the path towards the porch, from which the light streamed cheerfully out through the open door of the hall.

She was startled, when quite close to the house, to see a tall man standing outside the parlour window. The candles were not lit, but the firelight shed a soft glow over the room, and he was evidently absorbed in gazing intently in.

Marjorie's first impulse was to step across the grass and find out what brought him there; but before she could do this, he turned and went quickly past her, without seeing her, towards the garden gate. And a moment after she heard the sound of a horse trotting rapidly along the road.

Greatly puzzled, she went into the house. In the hall she met Tamsin, the old servant who had lived with her grandmother before her mother's marriage. The old woman's eyes were red, and Marjorie felt sure she had been crying. But this the old woman stoutly denied, and when Marjorie went on to tell her about the man in the garden, she declared that it must have been one of the men who were painting the stables.

"'Twas Ned Jones, I'll be bound, cheeld. It's just like his imperence, to be starin' in at the parlour winder. I s'pose he wanted to see what gentlefolks' rooms is like. Now, don't 'ee go and worrit Miss Nell by tellin' her. She's got a fancy for having the blinds up at nighttime. I'll talk to Ned."

Marjorie felt perfectly sure that it was not Ned Jones or any of the workmen. She had seen him clearly as he passed her, and the man was a gentleman. His coat and long boots were all splashed with mud, as if he had been riding fast, but he was unmistakably a gentleman. And though she could not understand how he came to be staring in at the window, his face was one to trust and like.

The Mystery Of An Old Murder

She promised Tamsin to say nothing about the mysterious stranger to Aunt Nell, but she was glad when, after tea, her aunt proposed that they should go up into her own room, instead of staying in the parlour, where it made her nervous to look out of the un-curtained windows at the darkness.

Aunt Nell's room was next to Marjorie's, and was, Marjorie thought, the most charming room in the house. This evening a fire had been lit on the tiled hearth, and sent a pleasant flickering glow over walls and ceiling. Miss Lane seemed in no hurry to light the candles, which stood ready on the bureau. She could knit by the firelight as well as by candlelight, she said.

Marjorie was glad of an idle time; a fireside talk with Aunt Nell was one of her chief delights.

For a time she talked merrily on, without noticing how brief and absent her aunt's answers were. But bending forward to give her back her knitting, which had slipped from her

hip to the ground, she was startled beyond measure to see that tears were dropping silently on her cheeks.

"Aunt Nell, you are crying! What is it? What is the matter?" she asked in keen distress and perplexity.

"My dear, nothing; nothing new. I have been

thinking of sad things that happened long ago, that is all," Miss Lane said gently. "I want to tell you about them, Marjorie. Before you go to St Mawan you ought to know. And I want to tell you."

Kitty's words instantly recurred to Marjorie, but she did not speak of them. She sat very still, waiting for her aunt to go on. Miss Lane only paused a moment.

"Has it ever seemed strange to you, dear child, that we have never visited St. Mawan, that you have heard so little about the place in which your father and mother were born?"

Marjorie shook her head. "No, I never thought of it, Aunt Nell, till—till—"

"I know. Kitty spoke to you. But you did not understand her?"

"She only said a word or two, Aunt Nell. I knew then there was some secret, but she did not tell me what it was. And I don't want you to tell me if you think I ought not to know. I will try not to think of it," said Marjorie, flushing up.

"My dear, there is no secret," said her aunt sadly. "We thought it too sad a story for you to hear while you were a child, but now I want you to know it. And first let me show you two portraits, darling."

She went to her bureau and unlocked one of the inner drawers. There were some letters there, and two oval miniatures, framed in gold. She brought the miniatures back to her seat and put one of them in Marjorie's hands.

"It is your great-aunt, Marjorie. I never saw her. She had married and had left St. Mawan before your mother and I were born. She never came back. She had married against her father's wishes, and he never forgave her while she lived."

"She must have been beautiful," said Marjorie, studying the portrait eagerly. It was the portrait of a young woman with flashing black eyes and delicately-cut features. Her powdered hair was brushed back from her forehead over a cushion, and hung in curls on her neck.

"Yes, her father was very proud of her. And when she ran away with Mr. Carew, it almost broke his heart. He was a changed man ever afterwards, I have heard my mother say. He was my mother's stepfather; Aunt Ellen was his only child."

"Was grandmother married when Aunt Ellen ran away?" asked Marjorie. She was still looking at the miniature she held; but she had begun to wonder whose that other miniature was, over which Aunt Nell's fingers were clasped so closely.

"Yes, she had married the year before. Aunt Ellen and grandfather lived at the Manor House alone together. Then she went to Plymouth on a visit, and met Mr. Carew. He held some good post in the dockyards there, and many people thought her father foolish to oppose the marriage. But he had heard things which made him dislike Mr. Carew and mistrust him, and he would not give his consent. And then Mr. Carew persuaded her to run away with him, and they went to Scotland, and were married at Gretna Green. It is quite a romance, isn't it, Marjorie?" and Miss Lane smiled sadly as she met Marjorie's eager glance. "But it ended badly, as such romances so often do in real life. She only lived six years after her marriage. She had several long illnesses and lost her good looks, and her husband neglected her. He was a very handsome, brilliant man, the idol of Plymouth society, and nursing a sick wife was not to his taste. Then he was angry with her because she would not try harder to obtain her father's forgiveness. He seemed to think that if she would go to the Manor House with her boy she would be received. But she knew her father better than he did, and was sure he would refuse to see her. And after six years she died."

"Was her father sorry then?" asked Marjorie

eagerly. "Did he make friends with Mr. Carew?"

"No, his grief made him still more bitter. For years he lived on at the Manor House alone, with only an old manservant to keep him company. We children used to be taken to see him now and then, and I remember how frightened I used to be at the big gloomy rooms and the silence of the place. It is a beautiful old house, Marjorie. You will see it next week as you drive from Bodmin."

"It is shut up now, is it not?" asked Marjorie timidly.

"Yes, I will tell you why presently. It has been shut up for years, my dear."

There was a change in Aunt Nell's voice, and her lips were trembling, but she went hastily on: "Grandfather was a rich man, though he lived like a very poor one. The estate is not a large one, though once the Vyvyans owned all the land about St. Mawan. But there was a tin-mine on the downs—it is deserted now. You will see the shaft of it surrounded by heaps of rubbish, overgrown with grass and heather. But in grandfather's time it was very productive, and he made a great deal of money by it. Then he made still more by his ships; he had a number, some of them used for smuggling, I fear. Everybody smuggled in those days in

St. Mawan. His great-uncle was called Miser Vyvyan, and after his death large sums of money were found hidden behind wainscotings and under the hearthstones, and in all sorts of queer places. And as grandfather became older the same love of hoarding grew upon him. My mother always believed he had a large amount of money hidden somewhere in the old house. I have heard her talking to my father about it, and saying it was not safe for him to live alone. That was before Robert came to live at the Manor House."

Marjorie looked up quickly. Even to her youthful ears the way in which her aunt uttered her cousin's name said a great deal. Miss Lane hurried on:

"You know who he was, Marjorie; Aunt Ellen's son. The land was entailed, and grandfather could not have willed it away from him. And when, after some years, Mr. Carew wrote, begging that his son might see the old house in which his mother had been born, and which was one day to be his own, grandfather consented to receive him, but on the condition that his father did not accompany him. He did not answer Mr. Carew's letter himself; his lawyer wrote. He was as determined as ever to hold no communication with him. Robert spent a month at St. Mawan that summer. He was just fifteen, and your mother and I were twelve. After that he came every year, and stayed longer and longer each time, till at last he really lived at the Manor House and only visited his father. I think Mr. Carew was glad to have him away from home. As was found out afterwards, he was deeply in debt, and had all kinds of difficulties about money-matters, which Robert knew nothing of. He was passionately attached to his father, and though his grandfather would not allow his name to be mentioned in his presence, he constantly talked to us about him. We were together a great deal. A day rarely passed without our seeing each other. Your mother and I loved being on the water, and Robert often took us out in his boat. Your grandmother never troubled about us if Robert was with us. She knew how careful he was."

Miss Lane stopped, looking dreamily into the fire, a faint, sad smile on her lips. Marjorie knew she was thinking of those happy days so long ago. She kept breathlessly still; not by a word or a look would she have disturbed her aunt's thoughts. But it was only for a moment Miss Lane paused. She went on in a steady voice:

"When Robert was eighteen he went to Oxford, and was there three years. He spent nearly all his vacations with us; grandfather was failing in health, and always grew restless and ill if he stayed more than a day or two, in Plymouth. And his father was more anxious than ever to keep Robert away from him. His affairs were in a desperate state; he had begun to be shunned by men of good position, and his most intimate friend was now a man named Baroni, who had lately come to Plymouth, and of whom very little was known. Robert disliked this man intensely, and it troubled him that he should be on terms of intimacy with his father. But he was as yet wholly ignorant of his father's bankrupt condition. Mr. Carew always spoke cheerfully to him. I think he really loved his son, and wanted to keep his good opinion. If he had only confided in him!"

Marjorie had moved from her chair and was kneeling by her aunt's side. She put her arm round her as she heard her voice tremble, and Miss Lane turned and looked down at her with sad, loving eyes.

"Darling, it is a terrible story I have to tell you. I will try to be as short as I can. The first time Robert learnt that his father was in great need of money was the autumn after he left Oxford. Mr. Baroni came to St. Mawan to survey some land which a company he was interested in thought of leasing for mining purposes.

"He stayed at the inn for a fortnight or more, and spent a good deal of time in exploring the coast. He joined us in some of our boating expeditions, and I have never disliked anyone so much. We were all very glad when he went away. Little things he had said to

Robert had made him very anxious about his father, and the next market-day after he left, Robert went to Plymouth to see Mr. Carew.

"There was no coach between Bodmin and Plymouth then, but Tregelles's van went from St. Mawan to Bodmin on market-days, as I dare say it does still. And Robert used to go as far as Bodmin in that, and then post on from there. That morning I walked along the cliffs with him for a mile or two, and then across the downs to meet the van at the top of Polruan Hill. It was a lovely, fresh, breezy morning; I can remember every step of that walk. As we passed Blackdown Point we saw a small schooner off the point, and Robert laughingly remarked that if he was a revenue officer he should keep a sharp watch on her. She was a stranger; we knew every vessel belonging to St. Mawan, and we had never seen this particular schooner before. But we forgot all about her as we turned inland. And I did not go back by the cliffs.

"That afternoon, as we were sewing in the parlour, Mr. Bulteel came in to tell us that Robert's father had just arrived in the town, and, leaving his horse at the inn, had gone to the Manor House. It was startling news, almost incredible; but Mr. Bulteel assured us there was no mistake. The landlord had talked with him for ten minutes or so. He had told him that Robert had started for Plymouth that morning, at which Mr. Carew had seemed greatly vexed. He had stayed the night at Padstow, he said, and thus had not met his son. Mother wondered whether she ought to go up to the Manor House; she feared the effect of such a meeting on grandfather, who was very feeble. But Mr. Bulteel persuaded her not to go, and, indeed, that afternoon she was not fit for the exertion, for she had been ill for days with one of her heart attacks.

"So we waited, expecting every moment to hear a knock at the front-door; for we felt sure that Mr. Carew would not go back to Plymouth without calling on us. Only the week before I had had a very kind letter from him. But just as the dusk had fallen Mr. Bulteel came again to startle us. Mr. Carew had gone without a word. He had gone into the courtyard of the inn and ordered his horse and ridden off at a gallop towards Padstow.

"Marjorie, I do not know how to tell you the rest. Grandfather had sent his old servant, and the girl who had come to help him since Robert lived there, into Bodmin that afternoon for some stores. When they got back it was to find the house dark and silent, and their master lying dead in the arched passage leading from the hall to the kitchens. He had been shot through the heart."

The Mystery Of An Old Murder

Marjorie's hands tightened their clasp on Aunt Nell's arm; she gave a low murmur of pity and horror, but did not speak. And it was a moment or two before Miss Lane could go on.

"Mr. Carew was never found, Marjorie. They traced him to Padstow; his horse was brought to the inn by a boy to whom he had given it just outside the town. But nothing further was ever definitely known. People believe he escaped to France, perhaps in that vessel we saw off Blackdown Point. And there was one fact that seemed to prove that it was to France he went. He had papers of great importance with him, relating to our coast defences, and these were afterwards found in the possession of French officials. They may have been stolen from him, he may have sold them. It was said of him that he had been a spy for years in the pay of the French Government, like his friend Baroni, who had had to flee for his life from Plymouth almost directly after returning from St. Mawan. But I have never believed that of him, Marjorie, never. Robert could not have loved him so if that had been true. He was passionate, and grandfather had a bitter tongue. They quarrelled, and he became mad with rage. It was no premeditated act. I have never believed it."

She gently loosed herself from Marjorie's clasp, and rose from her chair and moved away a few steps towards the window. Quietly as she had spoken, it had been a terrible task she had set herself, and now it was ended she felt faint and trembling.

She leant against the window and looked out at the quiet garden, pressing her throbbing forehead against the cool glass. Marjorie sat and watched her, her heart too full to let her speak. She felt she would like to throw herself at her aunt's feet and kiss the hem of her garment. How had she been so cheerful, so loving, when all the joy of her own life had been taken away?

Presently Miss Lane came back to her seat by Marjorie. She had something else to tell her, something Marjorie had guessed already. All the while she had been speaking she had been holding Robert Carew's miniature, but now she put it into Marjorie's hand.

"This is my cousin Robert, dear," she said gently. "I want you to see it." And as Marjorie bent down to look at it by the firelight she added, "We were engaged, Marjorie. We were to have been married in the following year. But it was not to be."

Marjorie hardly heard the last sadly-uttered words. She was gazing fixedly down, at the dark, handsome, vivid face of the young man in the miniature. Where had she seen that face before? She had seen it, she felt sure. And then it suddenly flashed upon her. The man who had been standing in the garden, gazing in at the window, was Robert Carew. He was greatly changed, all the youth had gone out of his face, but she was certain that it was he. And as she thought of him and Aunt Nell, the tears began to fall fast, and Miss Lane heard a little choking sob.

She bent quickly over her. "Marjorie, I shall be sorry I told you. Dear child, you must not be unhappy over it."

It was on Marjorie's lips to tell her that she had seen Robert Carew that afternoon, but she kept the words back. She remembered how he had hurried away. He had evidently wished to remain unknown, and she would not betray him. And before she could speak, her aunt went hastily on: "No one blamed him, no one could have blamed him. But he felt it right for us to part. And my mother insisted on it. He went away, and sometime afterwards we heard he had left England. I think he went to try and find his father. He would not believe him guilty, Marjorie."

Marjorie looked quickly up. "Oh, Aunt Nell, do you think—?"

Miss Lane interrupted her. "I fear there can be no doubt, Marjorie. Robert's love for his father blinded him. And perhaps by this time he thinks as we thought.

It is sixteen years since we saw him."

The tone in which she said this was quiet, but intensely sad; it pierced Marjorie's loving heart. She caught her aunt's hand, holding it close against her face with an inarticulate murmur of pity and love. Oh, if only she could do something to bring back Aunt Nell's lost happiness! If only the mystery surrounding Mr. Carew's fate could be solved and he could be proved an innocent man!

CHAPTER 4

MARJORIE LEAVES HOME

It was on a bright sunshiny March morning that Marjorie and her father started for St. Mawan. They drove to Driscombe in time for the early coach, which, however, only availed them for the first stage of their journey. At Tresco, a small town on the Plymouth

Road, Mr. Drew hired a post-chaise, and they drove by cross country roads to Bodmin, whence, as it was market-day, Tregelles's van would take them to St. Mawan, if Mr. Bulteel had not been able to meet them with his trap.

Marjorie was delighted with Bodmin, which seemed a sort of metropolis to her. As she walked up the long hilly street, past the town-hall and the numerous shops, she felt the same elation a girl feels now on seeing Regent Street for the first time. And her eyes were busy at work as they passed the windows of the mantua-makers, where the latest fashions from Plymouth were displayed. Marjorie was not over-fond of dress, but it gratified her to see that her pelisse was just the right length, and that her mother had been right in putting three instead of two ostrich plumes on her bonnet.

They were half-way up the street when Marjorie noticed a little crowd gathered round the arched gateway of the principal inn. They were waiting for the mail-coach from Plymouth, her father told her. It came in daily at this hour.

"Do let us stop and see it," Marjorie begged eagerly. "It may bring some news from the war, father."

The rector smiled at her eagerness, but was not at all loth to stop. He did not join the little throng of sightseers about the inn, however, but stood on the opposite side of the street, looking into the bookshop, where a tempting row of tall folios had caught his eye behind the small-paned windows; till presently there came the cheerful sound of a horn, and the mail-coach, the scarlet body and yellow wheels all splashed with mud, rattled gaily over the paved street and drew up at the inn, true to its time to a moment.

There was only one inside passenger, a man of middle height, with thin sloping shoulders. He got slowly out and went up the steps of the inn, leaning on his stick. He wore a pair of large blue spectacles, and was apparently in feeble health. One of the outside passengers was known to the rector, a prosperous individual with farmer written all over him, from the top of his low-crowned beaver hat to the thick soles of his high boots. He wore a blue cloth coat buttoned tightly across his broad chest, with a large white neck cloth above it, and a bunch of heavy seals dangled at his fob. He hailed the rector in a loud, cheerful voice, and while Mr. Drew stepped across to speak to him, to exchange snuff-boxes and discuss the last news from the Peninsula, Marjorie had time to watch the cheerful scene. The coach went no farther than Bodmin at that time, and presently disappeared under the archway, into the courtyard, to remain there till the time came for its return journey to Plymouth. The coachman and guard were both Bodmin men, and a great deal of friendly raillery went on in broad Cornish between them and their neighbours. The landlord in shirt-sleeves, and his wife with a spotless lawn handkerchief folded over her ample bosom, were at the inn door enjoying the fun, and occasionally taking part in it. Good-humour was in the air, and in those days people had leisure to be mirthful.

But there was a cloud on the rector's brow when he rejoined Marjorie. He had just heard from his friend

that Robert Carew was in England. He had been met in
Plymouth the week before by a cousin of Mr. Willyams,
and though he had said nothing about going to St.
Mawan, the rector felt it most probable that he meant
to return there. Mr. Drew was not by any means an
unsympathetic person, and he pitied his wife's cousin
from the bottom of his heart. But he wished he would
stay out of Cornwall. Now Nell had forgotten the past
and learnt to be happy again, he did not want her mind
disturbed. But he said nothing of Robert Carew to
Marjorie. He began to talk to her of the old friends to
whose house he was taking her.

"I hope you will see Mr. Paul's grandmother,
child. She is an old, old woman, and remembers the
death of Queen Anne. Just think of that!"

Marjorie opened her blue eyes wide at this.
Queen Anne's reign seemed to her to lie far back in the
dim, mysterious past. It was with a shock of wonder
she heard that there was anyone alive who could
remember even the end of it.

The Pauls lived in a delightful old house just
outside the town. Captain Paul had made the voyage to
India many times, and the parlour was full of all sorts
of curiosities he had brought home with him.

Marjorie spent a most interesting hour in

examining them, and in talking to Mrs. Paul. But she was hoping all the time that she would be able to see the wonderful old lady her father had spoken of, and she eagerly looked her gratitude when Mrs. Paul suggested that they should go upstairs to her grandmother's room for a few moments.

It was a tiny, shrivelled old woman in a high mob-cap and snowy frills who sat in the cushioned chair by the fire in the big cheery upper room. With her ebony stick and her gold-rimmed spectacles, and small sharp features, she looked, Marjorie thought, exactly like Cinderella's fairy godmother.

She seemed extremely pleased to see Marjorie, and it was only after they had talked for a little while that Marjorie found out she was mistaking her for her Aunt Nell. Her first impulse was to try to undeceive her, but she found that the old lady would not understand, and Mrs. Paul, in a low tone, begged her not to say any more.

"Let her think you are Nell, my dear," she said; "she was always very fond of her." And then raising her voice, she added : "Tell us about your visit to London, grannie, when you were five years old."

That visit had been a great event in the old lady's life, and though it had taken place nearly a hundred years before, every incident of it seemed as fresh in her memory as though it had happened yesterday. She described to Marjorie how she had ridden part of the way strapped to a pillion behind her father, but that after reaching Exeter she and her mother travelled by the flying coach that ran between London and Exeter, taking four days to perform the journey, instead of eight or ten like the old stage waggons, while her father and some friends rode on horseback, well-armed because of the footpads.

And then came the part of the story that was so wonderful to Marjorie. How when they reached the village of Kensington, where they were to stay, they heard the Queen was lying dangerously ill in her palace, hard by their lodgings. And that a day or two after their arrival, her father came quite early in the morning and caught her up out of bed, and carried her wrapped round in his cloak into the street, where there was a great crowd, and men with trumpets and banners, before the palace gate. And they blew on their trumpets, and all the people shouted "God Save the King!" And her father told her that Queen Anne was dead, and that now there was a king in England.

"She remembers it all quite well, father," Marjorie said to Mr. Drew as they walked down the street together. "But she believed all the time that I was Aunt

Nell, and that I had come in to market from St. Mawan."

"It is often so as people grow older, my dear," her father said. "They remember what happened when they were children, while they forget the events of yesterday. And your Aunt Nell always went to see her when she came to Bodmin."

Marjorie did not say anything more for a moment. She had a book under her arm, bound in brown leather; Mrs. Trelawny had given it to her, just as she was going downstairs with Mrs. Paul. The old lady had tottered across the room, leaning on her stick, and taken it out of the glass bookcase for her.

"I always meant you to have it, Nell, my dear," she said. " It belonged to the Vyvyans once, and you have the best right to it."

Marjorie had hesitated for a moment about taking it, but Mrs. Paul had whispered to her to do so.

"Give it to your aunt, my dear," she said, when they came downstairs. "I know granny always meant her to have it."

It was a copy of Paradise Lost; on the title-page was written "Jasper Vyvyan, hys boke", and underneath the date 1675, and what looked like a rude attempt at drawing some animal, followed by a row of figures. Marjorie had shown this to her father, but he did not appear to be interested. He was, in truth, a little vexed with Mrs. Paul for sending Nell the book. And he told Marjorie she had better keep it till her visit was over; it would do her good to read and study Milton's great poem. She should set herself a task, and read so many lines a day. And this Marjorie had promised to do. But she was really much more interested in the words scrawled on the title-page than in the book itself, and after walking in silence along the street for a little while, she timidly asked her father if Jasper Vyvyan had lived at the Manor House.

"It belonged to him, child," her father said, rousing himself from a deep reverie. "His portrait hangs over the chimney-piece in the hall. That was the Jasper who was squire in 1675. But there are plenty of Jasper Vyvyans in the family history; it was a favourite name. They will tell you about Black Jasper at St. Mawan. He lived in Elizabeth's time, and is still said to haunt Blackdown Point."

Marjorie would have been glad to hear more about this interesting personage, but Mr. Drew quickened his steps, saying they had no time to lose.

"Though old Tregelles is more often than not half an hour late in starting, he sometimes starts to the minute, so we must be in time," he added with a laugh. "He is a character, Marjorie, and so was his father, who drove the van before him. It was Tregelles's van in my grandfather's time, and I dare say long before. There have been Tregelleses in St. Mawan as long as Vyvyans and Bulteels."

They had by this time reached the inn, and as they passed it, the passenger who had arrived inside the coach came down the steps, accompanied by a boy carrying his bag. He had just reached the bottom of the steps when he gave a start on seeing Marjorie, and his blue spectacles slipped off, and would have fallen to the ground if he had not caught them. He hastily replaced them, but not before Marjorie had seen his eyes. Black, piercing eyes they were, curiously brilliant for an elderly man. She wondered why he found it necessary to wear those hideous spectacles.

"What a strange-looking old man, father!" she whispered when they had passed him. "He must be old, he stoops so; but his eyes were not old."

"I did not observe him, my dear," her father answered, in a tone that checked any further comment on the stranger Marjorie might have felt inclined to make.

The rector was a student of books and a deeply-learned man, but he lacked his daughter's swift powers of observation, and took very little interest in people he met unless they were brought into personal relations with him.

They reached the market-place as the church clock was striking four. Tregelles, a stout, gray-haired man, with a mouth that shut like a trap, and a long, obstinate chin, was already seated in his place, whip in hand. As the last stroke of the clock died away, he shouted out to the market-women standing about the van that "time was up, an' he didn't mane to stop no longer for nobody".

There was a rush for places, but before all the passengers were seated the stranger from the inn appeared, the boy rushing on before him to keep the van from starting.

For three strangers to be going to St. Mawan the same day was an event indeed, and at another time Tregelles would have been as much interested as anybody. But this afternoon one of his moods of sulky dignity was on him, and if he felt any curiosity about his unknown passengers he was careful not to show it. And almost before they had taken their seats the van began to lumber over the cobblestones of the market-place.

CHAPTER 5

CAPTAIN O'BRIEN

The van was full that evening, as it usually was. The wives of the smaller farmers round St. Mawan, whose husbands could not afford to keep gigs for them, were regular customers of old Tregelles—Uncle Tregelles, as they all called him, in the kindly fashion of west-country folk. The top of the van was heaped with baskets that had been full of golden pounds of butter that morning, and now contained the week's purchases of groceries and such few things as the farms did not provide for the thrifty households. The owners of the different baskets sat within the queer vehicle, many busily knitting as the old horse leisurely took its way over the hilly roads. But the knitters were as ready for a gossip as their neighbours, and the clack of tongues went merrily on, while many kindly, curious glances were cast at the three strangers sitting near the door.

Mr. Drew was a native of St. Mawan, but, as it happened, none of those in the van remembered him, and old Tregelles, who would have done so in a moment if he had heard his name, had been in too sulky a humour for the rector to care to disclose himself. So the pleasant shock of surprise which comes when a lively curiosity is suddenly satisfied, went through the van when an old woman who had been waiting at the crossroads to be taken up, hailed the rector as "Passon Drew", and elicited from him the information that he and Marjorie were on their way to St. Mawan, to stay with Mr. Bulteel.

After this only one of the strangers remained to be accounted for, and just before the van reached Polruan Hill, a long ascent, up which everyone was expected to walk, the curiosity of the farmers' wives concerning him was satisfied also.

Mr. Drew had given up his seat next the door to the stranger. He still wore his spectacles, but he had thrown back his heavy travelling cloak on entering the van, and his well-made coat and fine ruffled shirt showed him careful of his dress.

Marjorie sat opposite him, and had an odd feeling that he was steadily watching her behind those blue spectacles, though when she looked at him he appeared to be observing the landscape. He had a well-shaped face, but it looked like the face of a man at death's door, so bloodless was it, so painfully haggard, and the ugly scar which ran along one side of it added to its death-like pallor.

He had said a brief word of thanks to Mr. Drew for giving up his place to him, but did not speak again till they were close to Polruan Hill. Then he turned and addressed the rector.

"If you know St. Mawan, sir, you may be able to tell me if my cousin, Mrs. O'Brien, is still alive." His voice was very low and husky, and he spoke slowly, as if articulation was painful to him. His accent was decidedly un-English, though he did not seem to be a foreigner.

The rector, slightly taken aback at the sudden question, and not remembering for the moment who Mrs. O'Brien was, hesitated over his answer; but the fresh-cheeked woman sitting by Marjorie hastened to give the information asked for.

"Do 'ee mane Mrs. O'Brien to Sea Cottage, sir? Her died two months agone. My sister-in-law's cousin's darter nussed her. 'Twas brownchitis took her off at last, but sheed been a sufferer for years."

He bowed politely. "Thank you, madam. I feared she would be gone by this time." He turned again to the rector. "I believe I am her only surviving relative, sir, Thomas O'Brien, captain in the East India Company's service." The rector bowed, but Captain O'Brien went on before he could speak. "I have just returned from India, invalided after thirty years' service. My cousin has written constantly to me, but her last letter spoke of fast failing strength. I feared I should be too late to see her."

By this time every eye in the van was fixed on Captain O'Brien. His name was well known in St. Mawan, though he had never been there. Was not Mrs. O'Brien's little parlour full of the presents he had sent her; a set of carved ivory chessmen, gorgeous Eastern embroideries, tall jars with dragons painted all over them? Was it not the money that came from him which eked out her tiny income, and made it possible for her to save enough to be taken to Exeter to be buried beside her husband?

The woman who had answered his question before now addressed him again. "Her spoke of 'ee often, sir, an' oped to see 'ee. But her knawed at the last her'd have to go afore you corned home. Her was failin' all last summer. Ann, that's my sister's cousin's darter, as kind a maid as ever was, used to carry her down to the parlour till the day afore she died. Her liked to see the things you sent her, sir. An' her'd dust 'em her own self, ivery one of 'em. They're all safe to the bank, 'cept a thing or two her gived away."

Captain O'Brien had listened very gravely, and only interrupted here to say that he meant to distribute among her friends any trifles his aunt had left, a remark received with great favour by the farmers' wives present; and when a few moments afterwards the van was emptied at the bottom of Polruan Hill, they gathered in an eager group round old Tregelles to tell him who the strangers were, and what a pleasant and generous gentleman Captain O'Brien proved to be.

Tregelles never walked up the hill himself, though he insisted on all his passengers doing so. And he listened with crushing indifference from his high seat to the women in the road. He was secretly deeply mortified at not having recognized the rector, or guessed that the invalid stranger was Captain O'Brien. He felt his reputation was at stake.

"What be 'ee scramin' at me like that for?" he said contemptuously to Mrs. Johns, who had spoken to Captain O'Brien, and was allowed the front place by her excited companions. "I knawed Passon Drew the moment I set eyes on 'em. That's his darter. Of course it's his darter. Can't 'ee see the likeness to Miss Lane? Tell me what I don't knaw next time. Gee-up, will 'ee!" (This to his horse.)

"But, Uncle Tregelles," exclaimed Mrs. Johns incredulously, "why didn't 'ee tell us? An' did 'ee knaw 'twas Cap'n O'Brien?"

"O' course I knawed. Mazy Jane would ha' knawed. Isn't his name on his bag?" And the old man triumphantly pointed his thumb at the carpetbag behind him, on which he had just caught sight of the name O'Brien in neat brass letters on the lock. "'Twasn't my place to speak to 'em fust. But only a pack o' silly women would ha' wanted to be told 'twas Passon Drew an' the cap'n. Gee-up, can't 'ee! Do 'ee mane to stop here all night?"

And shaking up the reins Tregelles drove triumphantly off.

Mr. Drew had tried to persuade Captain O'Brien to stay in the van, though not quite sure whether Tregelles would allow it without a good deal of grumbling about the extra weight to his horse. But the captain preferred to walk, and he and the rector strolled up the hill together, while Marjorie went on in front, eager to get to the top of the hill and enjoy the wide prospect awaiting her there.

The others were still far behind her when she reached the top. Tregelles had overtaken her father and the captain, and had actually climbed from his seat to pay his respects. He was walking beside them, holding the reins in his hand, while the market-women in a little flock behind caught eagerly at any crumbs of conversation which reached them.

But Marjorie only gave a glance down the road. Her father had told her she would get her first look at the Atlantic from this point, and she looked eagerly round the wide horizon till in a cleft between the hills she caught a glimpse of misty blue, which made her heart leap. Marjorie's grandfather and great-grandfather had been sailors, and the love of the sea was in her blood. And though she had been familiar from her childhood with the quiet bays and inlets of the coast near Saltleigh, this was her first visit to the north coast. She had never seen the real ocean before, the mighty Atlantic, on whose wide waters Ned's ship was somewhere sailing.

She breathed a long satisfied breath as she looked about her. Though they were still some miles from the coast, the air was briny and invigorating. It blew straight from the sea, across a bare, rolling country that to some eyes would have been dull and uninteresting, but to Marjorie's was full of charm. There were scarcely any trees; the rough wails edging the road were of stone, overgrown with coarse grass and heath; the land was barren, and much of it was uncultivated. Anything more unlike the typical English landscape, rich with verdure, softly wooded, could hardly be imagined.

But the larks sang joyously above the barren fields, the gorse was in bloom, and Marjorie knew that beyond those bare hills on the horizon lay the wide ocean.

She was wishing that she could walk the rest of the distance instead of getting into that stuffy van again, when she caught sight of a trap approaching her at a rapid rate along the white undulating road. She watched it idly for a moment, and then, with a start, saw that the white-haired gentleman, sitting so very upright in it, was Mr. Bulteel. He took off his hat and waved it when he recognized her.

"There you are, Miss Marjorie," he called out as he came near. "Welcome to St. Mawan, little girl. Mrs. Bulteel and Kitty wanted to come with me, but the trap was not big enough to hold us all. Where is your father? Talking to Tregelles about old times, I expect. What do you think of the van, eh?"

He had pulled up, and was looking down at her with such kind, twinkling eyes, that Marjorie wondered she could ever have thought him a formidable person.

"I don't think people can be in a hurry in St. Mawan, sir," she said demurely.

The Mystery Of An Old Murder

He burst into a great laugh. "Tregelles is one of our institutions, my dear," he said. "We should as soon think of interfering with the high sheriff. But you shall get over the ground more quickly for the rest of the way. I meant to be in Bodmin to meet you, but could not get away in time."

He had helped her into the trap as he spoke, and now drove slowly forward to meet the van, whose creaking wheels could plainly be heard on the other side of the hill. And in a few moments Marjorie and her father were travelling at a rapid rate towards St. Mawan, while the van lumbered behind them in its leisurely fashion.

Mr. Bulteel had asked Captain O'Brien to take a seat in the trap, but he had preferred to stay with the van. He was afraid to venture in an open vehicle, he told the banker in his feeble, hesitating, half-foreign voice.

"The poor fellow looks as though he would soon be with his cousin," Mr. Bulteel said. He is hardly fit to travel."

"He nearly died on the voyage, he told me," remarked the rector. "But he thinks the air of St. Mawan will be good for him. He has settled to stay with Tregelles. Will he be comfortable there, do you think? I warned him the cottage was on the cliffs, nearly a mile from the town, but that seemed an attraction. He wants quiet, he says."

"Oh, he will be comfortable enough; Tregelles's missis is a capital little woman. And she'll be glad to have a lodger. It's lonely up there when Tregelles is away, and she's as timid as a hare. She told me the other day that she had heard Black Jasper screeching as she had never heard him screech before. She was sure summat was going to happen. Black Jasper is our ghost, Marjorie. Did you know St. Mawan had a ghost? He is said to wander about Blackdown Point at night when the tide is high, and howl in an agony of remorse. He pushed his brother over the cliff one winter night, the story goes, and his ghost is doomed to walk for a thousand years."

" When the tide is high the air rushes out of a hole in the caves below the Point, making a strange sort of cry," the rector said gravely to Marjorie. "You can hear it by day sometimes, as well as by night. But all such sounds seem louder at night, and the fishermen really believe the story Mr. Bulteel has just told you."

"We all believe it, my dear fellow," exclaimed the banker with his hearty laugh. "Especially on a dark winter's night, when the waves are going over Blackdown Rock. I shouldn't care to cross the Point then, I can tell you. And your explanation sounds very satisfactory; but did you ever hear it yourself by day, now?"

"Often," said the rector decidedly.

Mr. Bulteel did not look convinced. "Oh, you hear something, I grant you. That's your air in the cavern trying to get out. But at night — well, it sounds different, anyway. And it makes my flesh creep, as well as old Nancy's; I'll confess it. We'll ask Captain O'Brien what he thinks of it. Tregelles's cottage can't be more than half a mile from the Point. How long has he been back from India, Drew? Just landed, I suppose, as he had not heard of his cousin's death."

"Yes, he reached England on Tuesday. But he has been in Lisbon for some weeks. He landed there, not able to bear the remainder of the voyage to England. He seems to have missed his last letters, and had heard nothing from his cousin since November."

"I wrote to tell him of her death. But he must have left India long before my letter was written. It is a pity he could not have got home before. The poor old soul would have been so glad to see him. But from the way she talked of him, I expected to see a much younger man. What age should you say he was?"

"It is difficult to judge when a man has been ill,"

the rector answered reflectively. "And the climate out there makes one year count for two. I dare say he isn't fifty."

"Ten years younger than I am! He looks ten years older. What do you say, Miss Marjorie? You have a sharp pair of eyes, I can see. But look, you can see St. Mawan now. There, at the end of this valley."

Marjorie looked, and saw a line of roofs and a tall church tower on the side of a bare hill. The curve of the hill hid the lower part of the town and the little harbour, from which the fishing-boats went out.

"That tower is a landmark to sailors," her father said. "I must take you up there tomorrow, Marjorie. Your grandmother and grandfather are buried in the churchyard."

He was looking eagerly about him now, noting each familiar outline. And he and Mr. Bulteel vied with each other in pointing out objects for Marjorie's attention. But neither made any remark about the gray stone house that presently came in sight—a low irregular house under the ridge of the downs, with a belt of firs about it. It was the firs which first caught Marjorie's eye; they were almost the only trees she had seen since Polruan Hill was left behind.

"How beautiful those firs are!" she said; "but the

house looks gloomy with all its windows shut up. Whose house is it, Mr. Bulteel?"

"It is the Manor House," he answered, glancing at her father.

And her father said quietly, "It is your Cousin Carew's house, my dear. Some of it goes back to Henry the Eighth's time. The date 1512 is over the front-door."

"You would not think the house was close to the sea—eh, Miss Marjorie? But it is. Blackdown Point is just over the ridge there. And we all believe in St. Mawan that there is a secret passage between the house and the caves under the Point. What do you say to that, Drew?"

"It is probably blocked up by this time, if there ever was one," returned the rector, in a tone that implied, to Marjorie's ears, that he wished not to talk of it.

But Mr. Bulteel did not understand the inflections of the rector's voice as Marjorie did, and he went cheerfully on:

"Oh, there was one! Old Tregony told me only last week that his great-grandfather and half a dozen others once carried a hundred kegs of brandy from a sloop off Blackdown Point right into the kitchen of the Manor House. But they were all sworn to secrecy, and there is nobody now alive who knows how to find the passage."

"There is probably no passage to find now," said the rector quietly. "Damp and decay must have destroyed it, if it ever existed, about which I have always been incredulous. Do you see those mounds overgrown with grass on the downs, Marjorie? That was a mine once. There used to be an open shaft there, Bulteel. Has it been filled up?"

"We talk of doing it, but it hasn't been done," returned Mr. Bulteel, looking at Marjorie with twinkling eyes. "We don't do things in a hurry in St. Mawan—eh, Miss Marjorie?"

Marjorie was bound to laugh at his quizzical look, but her eyes soon went back to the deserted mine on the downs.

The Manor House was out of sight now, though the tops of some firs rose over the hillside, marking its position. The rolling downs stretched gently upwards to the skyline, against which showed those grass grown mounds that her father had pointed out to her.

They gave the scene a desolate look, and Marjorie was glad when the road made a sudden turn, and the valley broadened out before them, cheerful with scattered houses and garden plots. The town was now close at hand, nestling behind a grassy headland, which jutted out into the sea, forming a shelter from the fury of winter tempests.

Marjorie had a glimpse of a little harbour, where a number of fishing-boats lay moored, of a long line of frowning cliffs to the westward with breakers flashing white against them, of a great, dazzling plain of ocean, below a sky ruddy with the sunset. Then the houses closed the prospect out, and she was in the narrow High Street, eagerly wondering at which house they would stop.

CHAPTER 6

TREASURE-TROVE

Bulteel's bank was about half-way up the High Street, on the sunny side. It was a square, double-fronted house, roomy and comfortable, and had a large garden behind it. The front rooms on the lower floor were given up to the business, but there was a long drawing-room upstairs, with three windows looking on the street, that Marjorie thought was the most delightful apartment she had ever seen. The furniture and ornaments in it had nearly all come from France, Mrs. Bulteel told her, brought over by Mr. Bulteel's father in the days before the war; and the inlaid cabinets, and spindle-legged tables, and smiling Dresden shepherdesses took Marjorie's fancy amazingly. But better even than the room itself was the view from the windows. There was so much to be seen from them; not only the whole length of the little High Street—but at the bottom of the street there was a glimpse to be caught of the harbour and the brown-sailed fishing-boats and the line of frowning cliffs beyond, and between the gabled roofs of the opposite houses a bit of the headland was visible and a shining breadth of open sea.

She was sitting with Kitty next morning in one of the broad window-seats, while Mr. Drew talked to Mr. Bulteel in his office, and Mrs. Bulteel was busy in the kitchen.

Kitty had been spending a delightful hour in showing Marjorie her dresses and jewellery, and describing to her the gaieties of the past winter. But now her spirits had flagged again. Marjorie was not the eager, admiring, envious listener she had bargained for; even the account of the fireworks at an evening fete in Vauxhall Gardens had failed to rouse her to enthusiasm. And she did not seem able to understand how Kitty could like living in a town as big as London, or why she felt bored in St. Mawan.

"These windows are so cheerful," said Marjorie, wonderingly. "Why, Kitty, how can you be dull here? There must be something to see all day long. Look! I think the fishing fleet must be going out. I hope we shall get down to the harbour before they are all gone. Do you think Mr. Bulteel will be ready soon?"

Kitty yawned, stretching out her pretty feet in their sandalled shoes and white open-work stockings.

"I don't think I shall go, Marjorie; a boat is so disagreeable, and I shall be certain to get my feet wet."

Marjorie's bright face clouded over.

"Oh, do come, Kitty; I am sure you will like to see the caves. And perhaps we shall go into the Manor House. Father said he wanted to look at the portraits in the hall."

Kitty sat up briskly at this.

"Oh! I hope we shall go through the house. It will make my flesh creep, I know, but anything for a change. It has been shut up ever since the murder, has it not?" And then, seeing Marjorie's grave, disturbed look, she quickly added, "You know all about it now, don't you, child? There is no reason why I should not talk about it."

"I would rather not talk of it, Kitty," Marjorie said hastily. "Please let us not."

Kitty tossed her head slightly.

"Oh, very well! But I should like to tell you what Lady Trelawny said. She knew Mr. Carew, and she does not believe to this day that he did it. I heard her tell mother so. And she thinks Robert Carew ought to have lived on at the Manor House and married your aunt. I think so too. Why should—"

"Oh, please do not let us talk about it," cried Marjorie, her nerves quivering at Kitty's light, critical tone. "And there are father and Mr. Bulteel coming up the stairs. We shall start now."

Mr. Bulteel was going to take them to Blackdown Point in his boat. They were to explore the caves as far as the tide allowed them, and then were to leave the boat and walk up Blackdown Valley to the Manor House. Mr. Drew had heard from his host that there was an old woman in charge of the place, and he wanted to find out from her, if possible, if her master was coming to Cornwall.

The fishing-boats had all left the harbour when they got down to it, but they were still in sight, and even Kitty was forced to own that they made a picture worth looking at, as they stood out to sea, the sunlight glowing on their brown sails.

"There, Kit, show us something equal to that in Lunnon town!" cried Mr. Bulteel, who had not grown tired of teasing his niece. "Isn't it better than all your Vauxhalls and your Hyde Parks? 'God made the country, and man made the town.' Who is it says that, eh? A sensible fellow whoever it was."

Kitty's face had a little pout upon it as she bent over the boat without speaking. She hated being teased, and had found that silence was her best weapon.

"Kitty has a greater poet than Cowper on her side," said Mr. Drew, seeing how offended she looked. "Does not Spenser talk of 'Merry London, my most kindly nurse'? Our greatest poets have lived in or near London —Shakespeare, Milton, Dryden, Pope."

"There, Kit, that's one for you," laughed Mr. Bulteel. "I must believe it, as Passon Drew tells us so. How delighted old Tregony was to see you, Drew. He knew you in a moment. But he has a wonderful memory for faces. I have noticed it often."

They were now some distance from the town, sailing abreast of the dark wall of cliffs which ran to the south-west from the harbour as far as St. Mawan Point, a rugged promontory sheltering the town on that side as the headland did on the other. Marjorie had been very silent. She was sitting in the bows, breathing deep of the strong sea air, and letting her eyes wander at will over the glorious prospect before her.

A cry of delight broke from her lips as they passed St. Mawan Point, and the lovely line of coast lay before her, headland after headland, point after point,

The Mystery Of An Old Murder

as far as St. Ives Bay.

Mr. Bulteel was delighted at her enthusiasm. He had the Cornishman's pride in the beauty of his country very strongly developed, and poor Kitty, who was of Dr. Johnson's opinion, and thought a London street better to look at than the most beautiful country view, and felt depressed and frightened at those dark towering cliffs her uncle loved so, was reckoned by him as an empty-headed little Cockney, whose opinions deserved to be laughed at. But Marjorie was a girl after his own heart, and he took delight in pointing out to her the various headlands, and telling her the different traditions that clung about them.

But it was on Blackdown Point Marjorie's eyes fixed themselves most eagerly. They were now approaching it; she could see the gulls flying round the bare rocky islet, which had once formed the extremity of the Point, but now was separated from it by a space of foaming water. The Point ran out some distance, sloping gently upward, clothed with heather and short close grass delightful to walk on, and then breaking sheer away in a mighty cliff, impossible for human foot.

It was over this cliff that Black Jasper was said to have pushed his brother, and Marjorie shivered as the boat ran into the deep shadow behind the rocky islet, and she looked up at the towering heights above her. It

73

was only half-tide, and there was still a margin of yellow sand between the water and the rocks; Mr. Drew and the girls were able to land without difficulty. It was only when the sea was very calm that the Point could be approached at all by a boat, Mr. Bulteel told them.

"But nobody ever comes here now, though fifty years ago it was a rare hiding-place for smuggled goods. But there isn't a fisherman in St. Mawan now who will come near it. Since—" He was about to make some reference to Mr. Vyvyan's murder, but checked himself. "I dare say there hasn't been a boat here for years," he added. "Now you must be quick, girls, if you want to see the big cave. The tide waits for nobody."

Kitty hung back a little. But for her dislike to be alone with her uncle she would have refused to enter the cave at all. Marjorie understood that she was really frightened, and that her shivers were not all affectation, as Mr. Bulteel believed. She held her thin little hand tight in her warm strong fingers.

"I won't leave you a minute, Kitty," she said, falling naturally into the position of the leader and protector. And Kitty clung to her, glad to be taken care of, and forgetting altogether her attitude of patronage. And it was from that moment she began to be really fond of Marjorie.

The Mystery Of An Old Murder

The cave was entered by a narrow passage between high rocks, dank and green with seaweed. The passage was very narrow and low at first; Mr. Drew, who went in front, carrying a lighted candle, was unable to walk upright in places. But presently it grew higher and began to broaden out, and in a few moments they emerged into a great cave floored with fine yellow sand, and with a roof too high to be seen by the light of a solitary candle.

"There is another passage leading to a smaller cave," Mr. Drew said, as the girls clung together, looking about them in the shadowy twilight the candle made. "We will have a look at it if Kitty feels brave enough. What is it, Marjorie?" For as he was speaking, she had made a little exclamation, and moved slightly beyond him, still holding Kitty's hand.

"There has been someone here before us today, father. Look, here are footsteps in the sand."

"Smugglers!" exclaimed Kitty in a voice of terror. "Oh, let us go back! They may be here still, sir."

Mr. Drew was examining the footsteps by the light of his candle. He laughed reassuringly at Kitty. "Smugglers are not pirates, Kitty. But your uncle says these caves are quite deserted now. And whoever has been here must have gone out again. The tide is rising fast, anyone without a boat would be caught."

"There are no footsteps going back, sir," said Marjorie, who was examining the fine damp sand.

"There is another passage out, my dear, to the left there. But shall we go on to the other cave, or is Kitty too much afraid?"

"No-o," said Kitty doubtfully, holding Marjorie's hand tight. Then her good-nature got the better of her fears. "It won't take us long, will it, sir? I should like to go on."

"Bravo, Kitty!" said the rector; " a soldier's daughter and a soldier's sister should learn to be brave. Follow me closely, we shall have to climb a little."

A rough flight of uneven steps cut in the solid rock led upwards to an irregular, low-roofed cavern, much smaller than the one below. The rocky floor was perfectly dry, the tide never rose as high as this. But the air was heavy, and the strange stillness of the place made Marjorie shiver as well as Kitty.

The rector held the candle high over his head. "Do you see those holes in the rock up there, girls? Some of them lead to other caves. If there was ever a secret passage to the Manor House, its opening must be somewhere in this cave. I often looked for it when I was a boy, but never succeeded in finding it. The rock is riddled by holes, almost like a rabbit-warren. The smugglers must have known the right opening by some secret mark of their own."

He turned as he spoke, to lead the way out. As he moved, the light of the candle fell on a small round object close to the wall of the cave, making it glitter.

It caught Marjorie's quick eye, and she picked it up with an exclamation of surprise.

"Father, do look at this pretty thing. How it shines! It must be gold."

Her father examined it closely.

"Yes, it is gold, I think," he said. "It must be the lid of a snuff-box, Marjorie. How could it possibly have got here? Let us look about. We may find the box."

But further search went unrewarded, and presently Mr. Drew declared that they must linger no longer or they would be caught by the tide. Mr. Bulteel hurried them into the boat when they appeared, and it was not till they were safely out in deep water again that Marjorie showed him her treasure-trove.

He put on his gold-rimmed spectacles, and turned it over and over, examining it intently, thrusting forward his lower lip, and knitting his bushy white eyebrows, as if some hard problem had suddenly presented itself to him.

"It must be the lid of a snuff-box," said the rector after a moment. "Marjorie found it lying on the ground."

"Yes, it is the lid of a snuff-box," Mr. Bulteel said mechanically, without looking up. "How in the world could it have got there?" Then suddenly banishing all expression from his face, he gave it back to Marjorie, telling her to put it in her pocket, and began at once to talk of something else.

Marjorie was puzzled for a moment at the sudden change in his manner, but she would have understood if she had heard what he said to her father as they walked up the valley towards the Manor House. Marjorie had expressed a wish to see the deserted mine close at hand, and she and Kitty climbed up the steep heath-grown slope of the Point, Mr. Bulteel declaring he was too old for climbing, and should keep to the valley. He was glad to get a word alone with Mr. Drew.

"It is a curious thing about that snuff-box," he said. "I could swear it belonged to Squire Vyvyan, Drew. It was the one he constantly used, and it was missing from his pocket when he was found."

Mr. Drew stared at him. "How could it have got

into the cave?"

"That is more than I can explain. But it was his. Look at it again presently. It has the Vyvyan crest upon it, a dragon. We must show it to Robert. But he will tell you what I do."

CHAPTER VII

A VISIT TO THE MANOR HOUSE

The deserted mine was on the top of the downs, only a short distance from the Point.

It was a dreary spot, made still more dreary by the decaying timbers and the grass-grown heaps of rubbish, which spoke of a time when the place had echoed with the cheerful sounds of labour.

The girls went to the mouth of the shaft and looked into it. Marjorie dropped a stone, and it splashed into water far below.

"Come away, do," cried Kitty, dragging her by the arm. "I am frightened out of my life. It must go down to the middle of the earth."

Marjorie laughed at her, but she herself was glad to go; the splash of that stone had set her shivering. They climbed back over the grass-grown heaps and turned towards the fir-trees, whose tops rose above the hillside, marking the position of the Manor House. But they had only gone a step or two when Kitty again clutched Marjorie's arm.

"What is that? Listen, can you hear?"

It was a strange, long-drawn melancholy cry which Kitty had heard, a haunting cry. As they stood listening, it came again, though not so distinctly.

"It must be what father told me of," said Marjorie, after listening in vain for it to be repeated. "The air trying to get out of the cave."

But Kitty walked quickly on. "Old Tregony believes the Point is haunted," she said in a whisper, as if afraid to hear her own voice. "And I would not come here at night, Marjorie, no, not for a thousand pounds."

It was pleasant to get into the fir-wood, where the rooks were building their nests in the forks of the tall trees. The wood had looked gloomy to Marjorie from the road as she drove past the day before, but she found it was full of light and cheerfulness. A squirrel looked down at them with bright brown eyes as they passed, and then swung himself gaily away from branch to branch. Kitty had never seen a squirrel before, and she was delighted with the cunning little fellow. Then a couple of rabbits darted across their path, and hid themselves in the withered bracken that made a carpet of gold under the trees. And Marjorie's quick eyes espied a nest in a thick bramble bush that had already two speckled eggs in it. But for the fear of keeping Mr. Drew and Mr. Bulteel waiting they would have liked to linger in the wood; as it was, Marjorie found it difficult to get Kitty away from the nest. Grand scenery bored Kitty, and she frankly detested the sea, but the wood with its wonders fascinated her.

The path through the wood led to the lawn, beautiful even in its neglect, with its fine trees and deep velvety turf. But it was on the house the girls fixed their eyes, Marjorie's full of sadness. She was thinking that this might have been Aunt Nell's home, but for the terrible shadow on it.

It was an Elizabethan mansion, with wide mullioned windows and a noble doorway. It was built of gray stone, the mullions and doorway of granite, and the effect would have been cold and severe but for the warm reds and yellows with which time had enriched the cold hue of the stone, and the plentiful wealth of creepers.

The upper windows were shuttered, but those on the lower floor were open, and as the girls passed along the gravel terrace in front of the house, they saw in one of the rooms Mr. Drew talking to a little old woman in a mob-cap and red knitted crossover.

The Mystery Of An Old Murder

The great door leading into the hall was flung back, and as they approached it, Mr. Bulteel came out of the hall, an odd, worried look on his ruddy face, as if something had happened to puzzle him greatly.

"Why, girls, we began to think you were lost," he called out to them. "Well, do you want to go down a mine-shaft, eh? I'll drive you over to Wheal Lizzy tomorrow if you particularly wish it."

Kitty declared fervently that she never wanted to see a mine again. "And that shaft is a horrible place, Uncle James. Anybody might fall down it and never be heard of any more."

"Poor Kit, you wish yourself safe home in London again, don't you?" laughed her uncle. "But nobody is going to throw you down the shaft, you need not be afraid. But come in. Captain O'Brien is here, taking a look at the old house."

Captain O'Brien was standing before the portrait of Jasper Vyvyan, which hung over the mantelpiece, but he turned as Mr. Bulteel and the girls entered, and came slowly towards them across the shining oak floor, leaning on his stick. He held his hat in his hand, and looked much younger without it, white as his hair was.

He appeared eager to improve his acquaintance with Mr. Bulteel, and Kitty, at least, was charmed by his courtly manners.

But Marjorie could not put away her first unreasoning dislike of him. His deathly-pale face, with the long, livid scar that distorted the upper lip, drawing it up on the left side showing the teeth, at once fascinated and repelled her. And she knew what strange, piercing black eyes those blue spectacles hid. She felt they were looking through and through her every time he turned to address her.

She moved away as soon as she could, and wandered round the panelled hall looking at the portraits, while he talked to Kitty and Mr. Bulteel. An open door she came to, gave her a glimpse of an arched passage, panelled and roofed in dark shining oak like the hall. She stepped within the door to examine it more closely, and then hastily retreated, remembering with a shiver that this must be the passage in which Mr. Vyvyan's body had been found. But she had noticed the rich carving that ornamented each rib of the roof and each panel of the walls, and the date, sixteen hundred and seven, cut deeply in Roman figures above the doorway opposite to that by which she had entered.

She went back into the hall and closed the door softly behind her. The others were still standing by the wide fireplace; Kitty and Captain O'Brien were talking of the delights of London, and Mr. Bulteel stood a little apart, rubbing one hand slowly over the other, a trick of his when deep in thought, as Marjorie had already noticed.

She passed him without speaking, and stood looking up at Jasper Vyvyan's portrait. It was a dark, handsome face she looked at, strong, and yet full of sweetness. The firmly-closed lips looked as if they had the trick of smiling; the dark eyes were both keen and tender. It was a little like the miniature Aunt Nell had shown her, more like what Robert Carew might have been if life had gone well with him. Jasper Carew had been a man of thirty-five when this portrait was painted—years of happy prosperity lay behind him. And there was little in the portrait to remind Marjorie of the man she had seen for an instant in the Rectory garden.

Her attention turned presently to the carving of the mantel-piece, and after studying it for a moment or two, she turned eagerly to Mr. Bulteel, pulling out the lid of the snuff-box from her pocket.

"Mr. Bulteel, look at this queer creature on the box. Is it not exactly like those on the chimneypiece?"

Mr. Bulteel turned with a start.

"Eh, my dear?"

She repeated her words, putting her finger on one of the dragons, forked of tongue and fiery of tail, which appeared again and again in the carving of the mantelpiece.

She was holding out the snuff-box lid as she spoke, and Kitty stretched her hand eagerly for it.

"Oh, let me see, Marjorie. Why, it is exactly the same! Just look, Captain O'Brien."

She had taken it from Marjorie, and now held it out to Captain O'Brien. He gave a violent start at the sight of it, and his lips twitched. But he recovered himself instantly, and bent to look at it with polite interest, but without taking it from Kitty.

"What is it?" he asked. "It is prettily chased."

"Marjorie found it in the cave just now," said Mr. Bulteel, who was looking at the chimneypiece, and had not noticed his start. "It has the Vyvyan dragon on it. You will find the dragon all over the house. Come and look at the passage leading into the kitchen—the carving is wonderful. That part of the house was built by Black Jasper's son in James the First's time."

He led the way, and Kitty and Captain O'Brien followed him. But Marjorie had no wish to go into the passage again. She crossed the hall, intending to go out on the terrace, but before she reached the door her father came out of the dining-room, where he had been talking to Tamsin Richards, Robert Carew's housekeeper, who, with her husband, had charge of the house.

"Marjorie, will you come here a moment," he said to his daughter; "Mrs. Richards would like to see you."

The old woman took both her hands, looking eagerly at her.

"I knawed your mother and your aunt well, my dear," she said. "You'ra the very picter of your Aunt Nell—God bless her !—ain't she, sir?"

"We like to think so," said the rector, putting his hand on his girl's shoulder.

"An' your brothers be away to the wars, your feyther says," the old woman went on. "Drat that Bonyparte! It's my belief there'll never be no peace while he's above-ground. You've never been in St. Mawan afore, have 'ee, my dear? Would her like to go over the house, passen? It's all in order. Maister Robert could ha' come home any day an' found it ready for 'en."

"Your cousin Robert will be here next week, Marjorie," said the rector gravely, "but only for a day or two. We will not stay to go through the house this morning, Tamsin. Marjorie must come and see you again."

"Yes, do 'ee, my dear," the old woman answered. "It's main lonely here sometimes. Come an' have a cup o' tay one arternoon, an' bring the Lunnon young lady weth 'ee." She glanced back over her shoulder as Mr. Bulteel and the others came back into the hall. "Cap'n O'Brien is a nice-spoken gentleman, ain't he, sir? He came to bring me a silk handkercher, knawin' Mrs. O'Brien had allus been a friend to me. But it did give me a start to find 'en in the hall just now. I made sartain sure the door was bolted, but he'd found it open, an' jist walked in. It sent me all of a twitter to see 'en standin' there, but I felt as if I'd knawed 'en for years when he told me he was Cap'n O'Brien. Mrs. O'Brien was allus talkin' about 'en."

Kitty began to talk of Captain O'Brien as they walked down the narrow, heath-clad valley to the boat. They would meet him again that evening, she told Marjorie. He was to be at Mrs. Carah's tea-party. Mrs. Carah was his cousin's greatest friend, and she was going to help him to divide the ornaments and the other things Mrs. O'Brien had left. He had been to see her that morning, and to ask her advice.

"He wants everyone who knew Mrs. O'Brien to

have something in remembrance of her. Do you not think it is very generous of him, Marjorie?"

"Very," said Marjorie, as heartily as she could.

Mr. Bulteel turned sharply round to her. He had detected the grudging note in her voice. "Eh, don't you like our visitor from India, Miss Marjorie?"

Marjorie was slightly taken aback at Mr. Bulteel's quickness in divining her thoughts. "I have only seen him twice, sir," she said, evasively.

But Mr. Bulteel would not be content with her answer, and questioned her as to the grounds of her dislike. But Marjorie could not explain; and as soon as she could she escaped from Mr. Bulteel, running on to join Kitty.

Mr. Drew was slightly vexed with her. Marjorie was a child, and had no right to form opinions about her elders. And when she ran on, he made some remark to this effect. Mr. Bulteel shook his head.

"She hasn't formed an opinion, Drew; she is too modest for that. But the likes and dislikes of a quick-witted, innocent creature like that girl of yours are worth attending to. And you may laugh at me if you will, but I have my doubts about that fellow."

The rector stared at him. "About Captain

O'Brien?"

"Yes. I have a shrewd suspicion that my worthy old friend was mistaken about her cousin, that is, if he is her cousin at all! What proofs have we that he is?"

"But what has he to gain by imposing on us?" argued the rector, only checked in his desire to laugh by the evident earnestness with which Mr. Bulteel spoke. "Mrs. O'Brien left no property, did she?"

"Not a halfpenny. All he could claim are those presents he sent her and those he is going to distribute among her friends. But a respectable name is a valuable commodity sometimes. It may be his own name; I do not seriously doubt it."

"Why should you?" said the rector rather warmly. "What reason can you have?"

"None at all, I own it. And I don't doubt it. But why can he not speak in a natural voice, eh? Why does he walk like a cat at one moment, and the next moment want the help of his stick? And why does he pretend never to have been in France when he speaks with a decided French accent?"

Mr. Bulteel had stopped, leaning on his own stick, and his voice gathered emphasis as he went on, his bushy eyebrows working. Mr. Drew began to see that he was in earnest.

"Come, Bulteel, what do you mean to imply?" he said, a trifle impatiently. "Do you think he is a Bonapartist spy?"

The question irritated the banker. "It never crossed my mind. It takes a parson to be really censorious, Drew. What did occur to me was that smuggling is a profitable business. He wants a boat. He is coming to the harbour this evening to see Tregony about it. What does he want a boat for? And he means to go out alone in her. I told him it was mad of him to attempt it, not knowing the coast. But it is my belief that he knows the coast well enough. He dropped a word just now that showed it."

The rector was grave enough now. "Bulteel, there is more in your mind than you are telling me. You have more reason to suspect this stranger than I know of."

But Mr. Bulteel would not admit this. "I am an old fool, I dare say, Drew. I have told myself so often enough this last hour. But I am keeping nothing back that I know of. Perhaps it was Marjorie's finding that box of poor Vyvyan's which has upset me."

"Do you suggest that O'Brien dropped it?" asked the rector drily. "But you know that is impossible, just as well as I do. He could never have climbed down the

Point to the cave; he is not equal to it. And—"

"Of course he did not drop it. Though how it came there— But I am an old fool, as you are thinking at this moment, Drew. Let us go on. The girls are waiting for us."

CHAPTER 8

MR BULTEEL'S SUSPICIONS

Mr. Drew had to leave early next morning to be in time for the Plymouth coach. Mr. Bulteel drove him to Bodmin in his high trap, Marjorie and Kitty sitting behind, looking very gay in their best bonnets and spencers. Kitty had insisted on their wearing them. Her uncle had promised to let her have an hour for shopping in Bodmin, and she wanted to look the young lady of fashion she was.

A little distance from the town they met Tregelles. He touched his hat and gave some muttered answer to Mr. Bulteel's loud, friendly greeting, but his face had its most sullen expression, and he stood for a moment looking darkly after them. For years he had kept his savings in a couple of leather bags under the hearthstone, but quite lately he had been persuaded to place them in the bank. He was regretting now that he had done so. Some apparently chance words of his lodger had perturbed his mind greatly.

Captain O'Brien was a travelled man, a gentleman to be trusted. If he thought Mr. Bulteel too fond of his own pleasure to be properly careful of other people's money, his opinion was not to be disregarded. And Tregelles, after a last sulky look at the trap, tramped on, half resolved to draw out his savings and put them back under the hearthstone, where he could watch over them himself.

The girls thoroughly enjoyed the long drive. The horse was a good one, and though they stopped for more than an hour in Bodmin, they were home before one o'clock. It was the day the post went out, and after dinner Kitty sat down to write her weekly letter to her mother.

Marjorie's letters had been written the night before, and were safely in Mr. Drew's pocket. As he was only going to stop a night at Plymouth, her mother and Aunt Nell would get them more quickly from him than if she had sent them by post.

While Kitty wrote her letter, Marjorie sat on the window-seat with the Milton book Mrs. Trelawny had given her on her lap. It was open, and now and then she knit her pretty brows and read a line or two, dutifully trying to follow her father's advice. But her eyes constantly wandered away to the cheerful scene without; and presently the book slipped to the floor, as she leant forward to watch a chubby little lad in a Holland smock, who had evidently been down to the harbour with his father's dinner, and was proudly swinging the tin can that had contained it. Marjorie had a healthy interest in her fellow-creatures, young and old, and she watched the happy little chap out of sight with a smile on her lips. Then she picked up the Milton, scolding herself for her laziness. She opened it at the title-page, and the next moment she put the book hastily down again and ran out of the room.

"What did you forget?" asked Kitty, as she came flying back again. She put her pen down, studying Marjorie with a critical eye. "Was it your necklace? But you had it on."

"I went to get this," Marjorie said, showing the lid of the snuff-box. "Yes, it is exactly the same. I wonder what those figures mean."

Kitty came to her side and leaned over her shoulder "What funny spelling, Marjorie! But it is a very old book, isn't it?"

"More than a hundred years old. It belonged to the Jasper Vyvyan whose portrait we saw yesterday.

Not Black Jasper, Kitty; he lived long before. But it is this drawing I am looking at. It is meant for the Vyvyan dragon, of course."

"It might be meant for anything," said Kitty, looking at the snuff-box and then at the rough pen-and-ink drawing. "It is as much like a pig as a dragon."

"No, it is the dragon. That couldn't be the tail of a pig, and here is his forked tongue. I wonder what those figures mean."

Kitty yawned a little. "What is the use of bothering about it, Marjorie? I dare say they don't mean anything at all. And I must finish my letter."

She went back to her desk, but Marjorie remained intent on the figures. There were five of them in a row—1607 + 3. What connection could they have with that queer caricature of the Vyvyan dragon?

She was still bending over the book with the lid of the snuff-box by her side, when Mr. Bulteel came upstairs. He looked sharply at the little golden lid. "Marjorie, put that away," he said, in a voice so different from his ordinary one that she looked up in surprise. "I thought you had given it to your father. It belongs to your cousin Robert Carew. Let me have it, my dear. He is coming to St. Mawan next week, and I will see that he gets it." He patted her shoulder. "Does it seem too bad to take it away from you, little girl? You shall have something else instead of it."

Marjorie felt a little hurt. "I don't want anything instead of it, sir. But did it really belong to cousin Robert? I am glad I found it."

"It is his now, my dear. It was his grandfather's. And—" Mr. Bulteel checked himself. "But what have you there? Is that the old Milton Mrs. Trelawny gave you?"

"Yes, sir. I was trying to imagine what these figures and the dragon could mean. Mr. Bulteel, do you think Captain O'Brien knew Mr. Vyvyan?"

"Why, my dear?" he asked sharply.

"I fancied he might have known him and recognized his snuff-box. He started so when Kitty showed it to him. Did you not notice, sir?"

Mr. Bulteel's ruddy countenance paled slightly. He had been down to the harbour since dinner, and found old Tregony puzzling his brains to remember who it was Captain O'Brien reminded him of.

"I could ha' sworn I'd seed the cap'n his self," he said to Mr. Bulteel, thrusting his great brown hand into his hair, and staring at him in a hopelessly puzzled fashion. "But considerin' as how he's never set foot in

Cornwall afore, an' I've niver been out of it, I can't ha' seed 'en, I s'pose."

This talk had left a strange, terrible suspicion lurking in Mr. Bulteel's mind, and Marjorie's words tended to strengthen it. He stared at her for a moment, and then hastily recovered himself.

"It must have been your fancy, my dear. He has been in India nearly all his life, and could not have known the old squire. But let us look at these mysterious figures of yours. Do you expect to get a clue to the secret passage out of them? It might be a fine thing for your cousin Robert if you could. St. Mawan folks believe there's a mint of money hidden away there."

He tried to speak jokingly, but the attempt was a dismal failure, and after a cursory look at the book he went out of the room again.

"What can be the matter with Uncle James?" asked Kitty as soon as he had gone. "He is worried about business, I suppose. I have seen cousin Hollies look like that when things have gone wrong on the Stock Exchange. But you don't know what the Stock Exchange is, do you?"

"Do you?" asked Marjorie, looking up with such a sparkle of fun in her blue eyes that Kitty was forced to confess her notions about it were very hazy. Kitty was finding out that it was amusing to talk to Marjorie, even though she showed so little interest in the fashionable world, and soon got tired of talking about dress.

"There, I have finished my letter, Marjorie," she exclaimed, folding up the big sheet. "Come and sit by the window. Put away that book."

"In a moment," Marjorie said absently. She had laughed at Mr. Bulteel's suggestion that the figures contained a clue to the secret passage, yet she could not tear herself away from them.

Kitty stood before the long mirror for a moment, patting her curls, and shaking out the scanty skirt of her white muslin dress, and then went to the window.

"Marjorie, do come here. There is such a funny old woman driving down the street. I am sure she must have come out of the ark."

"In a minute," Marjorie repeated, without looking up. It had suddenly flashed upon her that 1607 was the date cut over the doorway in the panelled passage. The dragon might refer to the carving on the panels; but what did the 3 stand for? Had it any meaning at all?

"Marjorie, she is stopping here. Is she going into

the bank? No, she is coming to the house door. Do look at that queer fat pony. I wonder if Aunt Mary will bring her upstairs; not the pony, but the funny old woman who was driving it."

Marjorie put down her book in despair and came to the window.

A small, rather shabby pony-carriage was before the house door, and one of the bank clerks stood bareheaded by the fat pony with his hands in his pockets. A smile began to dance in Marjorie's eyes and curl up the corners of her lips as she looked down at the shabby equipage.

"Kitty, I know who your old woman is who came out of the ark. I saw her and the pony in Bodmin, and father told me who she was. It is Lady Barmouth."

"Marjorie, that old creature Lady Barmouth! She is lady-in-waiting to Queen Charlotte."

"Yes, father told me so. He said you would know in a moment that she was a great lady when she spoke. I hope she will come upstairs, Kitty."

It seemed a strange thing to Kitty that Marjorie should be so cool and self-possessed, while she, who had seen so much more of the world, should be trembling with shyness at the thought of having to converse with a real live countess. But Marjorie was too free from self-consciousness to be shy. And her mother and Aunt Nell had trained her too well for her to behave awkwardly in any presence, however august.

Mrs. Bulteel was in the dining room, and a moment or two elapsed before she brought the visitor upstairs. Lady Barmouth had come on business. She had her diamonds with her, the famous Barmouth diamonds. She wished Mr. Bulteel to take charge of them for a week. They were generally kept in the London bank, she explained to Mrs. Bulteel, but she had brought them into the country to wear at a ball the St. Aubyns were giving to celebrate their son's coming of age, and she could not sleep soundly at night while they were in the house. The leather cases containing the jewels were still in her hand when she came into the drawing-room. She had heard from Mrs. Bulteel about her young visitors, and she had expressed a wish to see them. She was a little old woman, dressed in a big straw bonnet and a brown cloak that was a good deal the worse for wear. But, as Marjorie had said, you knew she was a great lady the moment she spoke. Not that she was haughty or overbearing, or condescendingly gracious. She chatted away as familiarly and freely as if she had been a neighbour dropped in for an hour's gossip, but she was the great lady all the same, and the boldest could not have taken a liberty with her.

After talking to the girls for a little while, she opened the cases and showed them her diamonds. The white fire of the stones seemed to fill the room as she held up the necklace, smiling at the look of awed admiration in the girls' faces.

"Put it away, put it away, my lady," cried Mr. Bulteel laughingly. "I will lock them up in the safe at once, if you please. When do you want them—next Wednesday night? I will drive over with them myself."

Kitty's little head was full of Lady Barmouth and the diamonds all the rest of the day. She was too much in awe of her uncle to talk much in his presence, but that evening at Mrs. Carah's party, while most of the elders were at whist in the dining-room, her tongue wagged freely.

Captain O'Brien had declined to take a hand at whist on account of his failing eyesight. But he made himself very agreeable upstairs with the younger members of the party, and Kitty found in him an attentive listener to her gay chatter. She was telling him that Mr. Bulteel intended to drive to Barmouth House himself on Wednesday night with the diamonds, when a look she caught from Marjorie, who was helping Mrs. Carah at the tea-table, made her stop short.

"Barmouth House? Is that far from here?" asked

Captain O'Brien. "And is it really necessary to take precautions against thieves in Cornwall? I thought robbery was unknown here. But I suppose I am wrong. Will your uncle have the town constable as an escort? There is only one, is there not?"

But Kitty was no longer eager to talk. As soon as she could she slipped to Marjorie's side. "What made you look at me like that, Marjorie ?" she asked in a whisper. "Was it wrong of me to speak of the diamonds?"

"I do not think Mr. Bulteel would like it," Marjorie whispered back again. "I would not say any more, Kitty."

Kitty shrugged her shoulders and made a grimace, but she had learnt to respect Marjorie's opinion, and she was silent about the diamonds for the rest of the evening.

CHAPTER 9

ON THE KING'S HIGHWAY

It was a great relief to Mr. Bulteel to hear next morning that Captain O'Brien had gone to Padstow to buy a boat, and would be absent a few days. He had gone in the van,— Tregelles went twice a week to Padstow as well as to Bodmin,—and would return in it the next market-day, which happened to be Wednesday. There was to be a party at the Vicarage on Wednesday night, to which he had been invited, and the van would bring him home just in time for it.

The knowledge that he was no longer in St. Mawan lifted a great weight from Mr. Bulteel's mind; it gave him time to think what he ought to do. He found it, however, more and more difficult to decide this the more he thought of it, and when Wednesday came he was still unable to see his road clearly.

It had been a troubled, anxious week for him in

more ways than one. The dark suspicion which had taken possession of him, haunting him day and night, would of itself have been enough to render him irritable and moody and unlike himself. But business troubles came to add to his anxiety, and coming at a time when he was least able to bear them, their effect on him was out of all proportion to their importance.

In a tiny town like St. Mawan rumour thrives on the scantiest fare, and when Tregelles came back from Bodmin on Saturday night with the news of the failure of a Plymouth firm with whom Mr. Bulteel was known to have dealings, no one who saw the banker's altered looks or heard his growling voice but believed that his loss was far greater than it was declared to be.

On Monday morning Tregelles withdrew his precious savings from the bank, and replaced them with grunts of satisfaction in the leather bags under his hearthstone. He had insisted on having it all in gold; the old clerk, who had been in Bulteel's for forty years and more, stared at him as if he could not have heard aright when he refused the banknotes offered him. But Tregelles did not care how the clerk looked. "I can't afford to run no risks," he told his passengers on Tuesday afternoon in Bodmin market-place. And the farmers' wives had looked at each other with alarmed faces, each thinking of the little store laid up in the bank for a rainy day, or of the egg-and-butter money, mostly in notes signed "James Bulteel", hidden snugly away in the stocking-foot till rent-day came.

But "Bulteel's" had too firm a place in the confidence of St. Mawan for its credit to be shaken in a hurry, and though a few people besides Tregelles withdrew their accounts, and less was paid in than usual, nothing had happened to alarm Mr. Bulteel when the bank closed on Wednesday afternoon.

He started about six o'clock on his drive to Barmouth House. Mrs. Bulteel and the girls drove with him as far as the Vicarage, which was just outside the town on the Bodmin Road.

The old vicar was in the garden waiting to receive his guests. He came to the gate to ask Mr. Bulteel to get back as quickly as he could.

"Supper is at nine o'clock; there'll be time for a rubber after that if you're not late," he told him. The vicar loved a good game of whist, and the banker was an opponent worth having.

"I shall be back before nine, never fear," Mr. Bulteel promised. "Teazer has not been out of the stable today. He'll not let the grass grow under him."

At the rate the trap went up the quiet valley road

it did not seem likely that the vicar would be kept waiting for his rubber. Mrs. Bulteel looked after it with a shade of anxiety on her placid face. She wished that her husband would have done what she had asked him to, and taken Prior, his head clerk, or one of the younger ones, with him. It was a lonely drive to Barmouth House, along the highroad as far as Polruan Hill and then by an unfrequented crossroad. She laughed at her own fears the next moment, and was ready to be keenly interested in the vicar's tulips, as she and the girls went round the garden with him in the twilight.

But the time seemed to go very slowly, and as she played whist in the parlour after tea she found herself listening breathlessly to the old clock in the hall as it struck the hours and half-hours in its deep mellow notes. She was not a nervous woman, but an indefinable sense of danger oppressed her that evening. And she longed with painful intensity for her husband's return.

Kitty and Marjorie were the only young people in the party, and Kitty found it decidedly dull. Even Captain O'Brien, when he came, preferred cards to conversation with her, and joined the vicar and Mrs. Bulteel and Mrs. Carah at a game of whist.

But he played carelessly, and the vicar, who, like

Mrs. Battle, loved "the rigour of the game", began to eye him with deep disfavour as the game went on. The old vicar had a nature as sweet and sunny as a child's, except at the card-table. But a partner who trumped his best card and forgot to follow his lead roused a bitter animosity in him, and only the remembrance that Captain O'Brien was a guest in his own house prevented him from uttering the scathing sarcasms that rose to his lips. He gave up his place as soon as he could, and devoted himself to amusing Kitty and Marjorie, whom he found looking at a portfolio of old prints and drawings his wife had found for them.

Kitty had been yawning dismally over them, but Marjorie soon became interested when she discovered that many of them were cleverly executed drawings of the Manor House, from different points of view.

"Ah! my sister did those, thirty years ago and more," the vicar said, glancing at them. "You have seen the old house, haven't you, my dear?"

"Only the front and the hall and the panelled passage," said Marjorie, hesitating a little.

The vicar gave her a quick, kind glance. He understood why she had faltered. But he made no reference to the mystery whose shadow still lay so darkly over the old house. He went on speaking of the drawings. "That is the sun-dial in the garden at the back of the house. Go and look at it when you are in the house again. It is older than the house itself. And here is a drawing that will interest you still more. It is a bit of the old castle that was pulled down to build the present house."

Both Marjorie and Kitty looked with interest at the little sketch of the ruined gateway, its mouldering stones wreathed thickly with ivy. "It was pulled down by Squire Vyvyan; the foundations gave way, and it became dangerous. But some of the granite blocks in it were used in building the summer-house. It is easy to distinguish them; each one has the Vyvyan dragon cut in it—three of them, just as on the shield of Sir Gilbert Vyvyan in Ladrock Church. Probably all the granite blocks in the old castle were stamped in the same manner. You will find a few of the old stones in the present building, if you look for them. There is one near the kitchen door, close to the panelling. It is worn down, but by looking closely you can just make out the tails of two of the dragons and the head of the other."

Marjorie was hanging on his words with breathless interest, and the announcement of supper at that moment came as a most unwelcome interruption. She had been about to speak of that puzzling row of figures in the title-page of the Milton. Did that 3 with the tiny cross before it refer to the stone with its three dragons, which the vicar had spoken of as near the door above which the date 1607 was carved? She was eager to know what the vicar thought, and determined to ask him as soon as an opportunity offered itself.

At supper she was seated at Mrs. Fortescue's end of the long table, next Captain O'Brien and opposite Mrs. Bulteel. She noticed how pale and anxious Mrs. Bulteel was looking, and suddenly found herself listening with a beating heart for the sound of wheels on the road, though till that moment no thought of danger had associated itself in her mind with Mr. Bulteel's journey.

It seemed as if that indefinable foreboding which had seized on Mrs. Bulteel was now laying its chill grasp on the rest of the company.

Before the end of the meal the conversation began to languish, and though no one spoke of Mr. Bulteel, except to suggest in cheery tones some plausible excuse for his late arrival, his appearance would have been hailed with intense relief.

Captain O'Brien had appeared greatly disappointed at not finding Mr. Bulteel at the Vicarage when he arrived, and he asked Marjorie several questions at supper as to the direction in which

The Mystery Of An Old Murder

Barmouth House lay, and its distance from St. Mawan.

"I am anxious to ask Mr. Bulteel's advice about a boat I am thinking of buying," he said in his gentle, hesitating voice, which most people found so pleasant, but which always set Marjorie's nerves on edge. "I must decide tomorrow morning. I felt sure I should find Mr. Bulteel here, especially as I was a little late in arriving. I missed my way on the downs. My eyes do not serve me well."

Marjorie did her best to answer him politely, but she was glad when they rose from table, and she could escape from further conversation with him. She went back to the portfolio of drawings in the drawing-room, and Kitty presently joined her.

"They have sat down to whist again," she whispered with a pout. "How long will it be before we shall be able to go home, Marjorie? This is duller than Mrs. Carah's party. Just look behind you. How dismal they all look, staring at their cards! Captain O'Brien is the only one who wants to talk, and Mr. Carah is frowning at him."

"They will hear you, Kitty," Marjorie whispered, not venturing to turn round.

"No, they are too busy. Poor Captain O'Brien, I am sure he must be bored to death. I wish Uncle James would come and take his place, then he could talk to us. But he has a very bad memory, Marjorie. He ought to have known Uncle James would not be here till late. You scolded me for telling him about the diamonds, do you remember?"

"Could a country mouse venture to scold a town one?" said Marjorie, her eyes dancing as she looked at Kitty. "I wish the vicar would come in, Kitty. I want to ask him about that dragon stone."

Kitty yawned. "Do think of something more lively than that, for goodness' sake, Marjorie. I am half-asleep as it is."

Marjorie was beginning some merry reply when she heard Mrs. Bulteel speaking to her, and turned quickly round.

"Marjorie, I have left my spectacles in the dining-room. Will you fetch them for me, my dear?"

Marjorie went quickly on her errand. She opened the dining-room door, and then drew hastily back. The vicar was just inside, talking to a tall, dark-haired man, who was carrying his hat in his hand.

The vicar would not let her go. "Come in, my dear. This is your cousin Robert, Marjorie."

He drew her in, and shut the door behind. her.

He was very pale and excited, but Marjorie did not notice that in her trembling eagerness, as she put her little hand into Robert Carew's and looked up at him. He held her hand tightly for a moment, but he had no time to speak. Mr. Fortescue went rapidly on:

"He has brought us bad news, my dear. We must break it to Mrs. Bulteel as best we can. No, it is not as bad as that," he added quickly, as Marjorie turned a terrified white face upon him. "But Mr. Bulteel has been robbed of the diamonds. and badly hurt into the bargain. Your cousin found him lying senseless on the road, half-way between this and Polruan Hill. His horse, poor old Teazer, dead beside him — shot, and the diamonds gone."

"He is at the Manor House," her cousin said gently. His grave, kind voice gave Marjorie back her courage. She had leant back against the door, feeling sick and faint with the sudden shock. But now she stood upright, looking at him with steady eyes, ready to help. He smiled at her. Even in that moment or two they had become friends. "Mrs. Bulteel must go to him," he went on. "I have sent for the doctor, but I am sure there is no reason for alarm. He was able to ride to the house with my help."

After a moment's consultation it was decided that Marjorie should make some excuse for calling Mrs.

Bulteel out of the room, and then while Robert spoke to her the vicar should tell the others. The country must be scoured to catch the thief.

CHAPTER 10

THE CRY FROM THE CLIFFS

The news that Mr. Bulteel had been robbed of the diamonds caused a profound sensation in St. Mawan. Highway robbery was almost unknown in Cornwall, and to hear of a masked highwayman on the Bodmin Road would have been enough to thrill the most stolid, even if his victim had been a far less important person than the banker, and the booty he had carried off a few guineas, instead of the famous Barmouth diamonds.

Next day the quiet High Street was crowded with country people, who had come in to find out all that was known of the mysterious affair. "Anybody would think 'twas Whitsun Fair," the old constable from Bodmin said to Captain O'Brien as they went up the street together to the bank, where the vicar and Robert Carew, and one or two other gentlemen who had been engaged all night in searching for the thief, were holding a council of war.

Captain O'Brien had remembered noticing a man with red hair and narrow shoulders, corresponding to the banker's confused description of the thief, lurking under a high hedge near Polruan Church Tower, and the constable had been endeavouring to follow up this clue. But nothing had come of it; no red-haired man had been seen in the neighbourhood. If the ground had opened and swallowed him up, the highwayman could not have disappeared more completely.

Captain O'Brien repeated what the old constable had said about the street looking as if it was fair-time to the vicar as they stood together at the drawing-room window.

Mr. Fortescue shook his head and sighed anxiously as he looked down at the crowd below. It had thickened round the bank, and there was much coming and going through the open doors.

"They are in no holiday humour," he said in a low voice. "I fear this is going to be a bad business for poor Bulteel."

"Oh, I hope not!" returned Captain O'Brien cheerfully. "He will be well again in a week or two, the doctor thinks. And we shall get the diamonds back. The man will be caught, never fear. He is bound to be."

The Mystery Of An Old Murder

"But too late maybe to save the bank, unless he is taken in the next few hours," said the vicar gloomily. "Look at the faces down there, O'Brien. Do you see that woman pressing through the crowd with a bundle of notes in her hand. I know her well. She is the most gentle, timid creature in the parish. But she would try to tear down the doors with her naked hands if they shut just now. She is mad with fear. And fear is catching."

Captain O'Brien peered down at the crowd through his spectacles, and then turned to the vicar, his face very grave. "Then you fear a run on the bank?" he said, sinking his voice to a whisper.

The vicar nodded. "It has begun," he said. "Luckily it is three o'clock already, and there is the night before us. Carew is off to Plymouth. We shall all do what we can, but I am afraid of tomorrow."

Captain O'Brien had given a quick glance over his shoulder as the vicar mentioned Robert Carew, who had just come into the room.

"Mr. Carew has been absent some years, I think," he said. "It is strange that he should have found Mr. Bulteel. Mrs. Carah has told me his sad story. Your Cornwall is not at all the quiet, innocent place I always thought it."

Mr. Fortescue made some hasty answer, but he was not in the mood to talk of anything but what was uppermost in his thoughts; he moved back into the room to say a last word or two to Robert Carew, who was just on the point of starting with one of the bank clerks on his long drive to Plymouth. Captain O'Brien remained at the window, engaged in watching the crowd below. He did not turn round till Robert Carew had gone.

The clerk was waiting with the trap at the Manor House. It was thought best that as little as possible should be known of this journey to Plymouth, as it amounted to a confession that the bank was in danger.

Robert Carew left the bank by the side-door, and walked through the long garden to a gate that led directly to the green fields behind the town. He walked quickly, looking neither to right nor to left. For the moment, he had put his own troubles away from him. His dark eyes had a steady brightness in them, his firm lips were closely locked together. If "Bulteel's" could be saved, he meant to save it. He had not forgotten what Mr. Bulteel and his wife had been to him in his hour of trial.

He crossed the fields at the back of the Vicarage, and after following the highroad for a time, turned up a narrow grass-grown lane, which led out on the downs not far from the deserted mine. It gave him a start when he was nearly at the top of the lane, to see Marjorie running lightly across the downs above him, her straw bonnet in her hand, and her fair curls tossed in the wind. She did not see him at once, and he watched her with a paling cheek. It was as if the past had come back again, and Nell was there before him in her beautiful youth. The girl he had loved in that other life was no longer first with him. The image he held enshrined in his heart of hearts was that of a woman with sad eyes and sweet smiling lips, whom, unseen, he had watched from outside the Vicarage window. But to see Marjorie so suddenly thrilled him in every nerve. He had not realized, the night before, the wonderful likeness she bore to her aunt. She came quickly down the slope to meet him. She and Kitty were staying at the Vicarage, but she had been at the Manor House since dinner, sitting with Mr. Bulteel, who had insisted on coming downstairs that morning, though he still seemed dazed and confused, and had no very clear recollection of what had happened the night before.

"Have you seen Mrs. Bulteel, cousin Robert?" she asked. "She has gone to the bank. She hoped to find you there."

He looked troubled. "No, I have not seen her. I am sorry she has gone into the town, Marjorie. Are you going to the Vicarage?"

"No, I am taking a letter to Mr. Prior, which Mr. Bulteel forgot till now. Cousin Robert, why do you wish Mrs. Bulteel had not gone into the town? Is there something wrong at the bank? Mrs. Richards said something to me just now which made me think there might be."

"Yes, there is something very wrong," he said, gravely. "A run has begun on it. Do you know what that means, Marjorie? All the people who have money in the bank want it out at once, and it is difficult to pay them. Go after Mrs. Bulteel, dear. Persuade her to come back with you."

She asked him no more questions, and would have hastened at once to do his bidding, but he spoke again very quickly. "Tell her I shall be back without fail before the bank opens tomorrow. I am going to Plymouth; they can give us no help worth speaking of at Padstow or Bodmin. When people go mad with fear, as they are doing now, Marjorie, nothing but actual golden sovereigns will satisfy them. Even Bank of England notes will not. And the gold that was stored in the bank cellars this morning is nearly all gone."

"But can you be back from Plymouth in time?" she asked in a very anxious, wondering voice. His manner showed her how real the danger was.

"Yes, I shall be back," he said confidently. He wished he could have felt as sure that he would bring the gold that meant safety to the bank with him, but he did not say this aloud. "Tell Mrs. Bulteel that I am certain to be back, Marjorie. Do not go through the High Street. Go across the fields to the garden door."

He hurried away, and Marjorie went down the lane towards the Vicarage fields. She would have much preferred to continue her walk across the downs and along the harbour to the High Street. But her cousin Robert was a person to be obeyed. She felt quite sure that he had good reason for all he said. Marjorie did not give her trust lightly, but she had given it unreservedly, and at once, to this grave, strong man, whose very voice had such help and comfort in it.

She walked quickly across the fields, and soon reached the door leading into the long garden, a green, beautiful place, fragrant with violets this sweet March afternoon. No sound but the singing of the birds greeted her as she entered it; but on approaching the house a dull murmur reached her from the street, the murmur of many voices, and through the iron railings of the little paved court at the side of the house she could see that the street was crowded.

The dining-room had a French window opening on the garden. Marjorie passed through this, half expecting to find Mrs. Bulteel in the room. But she was not there, and Marjorie went to seek her upstairs. Just outside the dining-room was a green baize door, cutting off the rooms used for the bank from the rest of the house. Close to this door Mrs. Bulteel was standing, clutching the door-handle with both hands as she bent to listen. She turned with a start as Marjorie opened the dining-room door. Her round face, that seemed meant for smiles and happy looks, was pinched and drawn, and the colour of ashes. She did not speak, but holding up her hand for Marjorie to be silent, bent again to listen. The sound of tramping feet came from the outer office; people seemed to be ceaselessly coming and going. As Marjorie listened, holding Mrs. Bulteel's hand tight, she began to tremble, she hardly knew why. Suddenly above the sound of the footsteps came the clear voice of the church clock striking four. Mrs. Bulteel drew herself upright with a low sobbing breath, and then, as she heard the heavy doors swing to, and the great iron bolts slide into their places, she burst into tears, hiding her face against Marjorie's shoulder.

Marjorie drew her into the dining-room, soothing her as if she had been a child. And Mrs. Bulteel clung to her, weeping. But she composed herself, and hastily dried her eyes as she heard the baize door open.

The Mystery Of An Old Murder

"It is Mr. Prior, my dear," she said to Marjorie hastily.

The old clerk came in, his face as white as his neck cloth. The vicar and Lord Barmouth's steward were with him. They had come to ask Mrs. Bulteel if she thought her husband had recovered sufficiently to be told the serious position the bank was in. If the run upon it had begun an hour earlier, it would have had to stop payment that afternoon.

Marjorie slipped away into the garden, feeling that she was not wanted. She found old Tregony roaming aimlessly about, his brown, wrinkled face the picture of consternation.

"The folks must be mazed, my dear," he said to Marjorie, in a voice full of angry bewilderment. "I've bin tellin"em so. They'm like a pack o' silly sheep. Hearken to 'em out there. Do they think the bank's goin' to disappear afore tomorrer mornin'? Drat 'em, like the duckin' of a few of 'em in Perran Pool. Do 'ee knaw what they'm sayin' now, miss? That the maister niver met no high-wayman at all! Did 'ee ever hear o' sich ungrateful folks, arter all the maister's done for 'em. But they'm mazed."

Marjorie was staring at him, not able to understand. "What do they say, Tregony?" she asked.

"'Taint no wonder you'm muddled, my dear. It takes fools and knaves to think o' sich lies. But that's what they'm sayin'; that the maister's got the diamonds hisself an' manes to run off with 'em an' the money in the bank. Catch 'em sayin' it to me. My missus heard Tregelles a-talkin' of it. That lodger of his put 'en up to thinkin' sich wicked stuff, I'll be bound. I met 'en coming down the strate just now, smilin' to hisself as though 'twere all a bit o' play-actin' got up to amuse 'en."

Marjorie hardly heard these last words. "Tregony, they can't believe such a thing of Mr. Bulteel," she exclaimed, almost inclined to laugh, yet thrilled with indignation.

"My dear, they'm mazed," the old man repeated in a tone of intense bitterness. "But I'm goin' out to talk to 'em again. I come in here to cool down a bit. 'Taint no good to try to argy with a pack o fools if you can't kape your temper."

He went off, and after a few moments Marjorie saw Mrs. Bulteel coming to her from the house. She was not alone. Lady Barmouth was with her.

The countess shook hands with Marjorie and smiled encouragingly at her. "Get the colour back into your cheeks, my, child. I am going to do some shopping in the town, and I want you and Mrs. Bulteel to come with me." She tapped Marjorie's cheek. "Run up to your room and put a tippet on. It is getting chill, and we shall have to drive slowly. All the world seems to be in the High Street this afternoon."

Mrs. Bulteel had shrunk in painful distress from the thought of appearing in the crowded street, but Lady Barmouth was determined to have her way, and she had been forced to submit, especially as the vicar and Mr. Prior both urged her to accept the countess's invitation. They knew why Lady Barmouth was anxious that St. Mawan should see her and Mrs. Bulteel together, and after her talk with old Tregony Marjorie knew too.

They drove to the top of the street and then down, calling at several shops. Lady Barmouth would have driven up the street again, but a glance at Mrs. Bulteel's face made her alter her mind. The banker's wife had done her best to follow Lady Barmouth's advice and look as if her mind was perfectly at ease, and the crowd in the street a mere holiday crowd having nothing to do with the bank. She had sat perfectly upright, with her trembling hands hidden under the fur carriage-rug, smiling at intervals when Lady Barmouth addressed her, though not attempting to speak much. But it was a dreadful ordeal for her to be stared at by hard, suspicious eyes, to feel that those pale-faced men and women in the crowd, who yesterday were friends and neighbours, were ready now to ruin her husband in their selfish terror.

After that sharp glance at her face, Lady Barmouth pulled her pony up. "We will go back to the Manor House," she said. "But I want to see Captain O'Brien, who seems to be the only person who caught sight of that wretched thief. Do you know Tregelles's cottage, my dear?" she added, turning to Marjorie. "Could you take a message for me? Say Lady Barmouth is at the Manor House and would be glad to see Captain O'Brien."

It was nearly six o'clock, and the sun had set. The day had been a beautiful one, sunny and spring-like; but it was now cold and misty, and Marjorie walked fast up the winding path which led from the harbour to the downs. Tregelles's cottage was on the downs, about half-way between St. Mawan and Blackdown Point. When Marjorie reached the top of the path she could plainly see the bare, dreary little house, but by the time she had walked a quarter of a mile it was completely hidden from her. The wind had risen, bringing with it a white blinding fog, that, like a curtain suddenly falling, blotted out the landscape.

It was only very slowly, and with great difficulty,

that Marjorie was able to make any progress at all. Luckily the path was clearly marked, a narrow ribbon of smooth green turf between thickly-growing heath and gorse. She made her way step by step, stopping now and again to listen to the sound of the breakers to be sure that she was moving away from the sea instead of towards it. It was high tide, and she could distinctly hear the dull, thunderous roar of the great waves as they broke against the cliffs. Once or twice as she stopped to listen, she could distinguish a fainter, shriller sound, which she knew must be the cry she and Kitty had heard from the Point, Black Jasper's cry.

She had laughed at Kitty's fears then, but now her own cheek grew pale and her knees shook. It was in vain she remembered what her father had told her, that it was nothing but the air in the cavern trying to get out; the cry thrilled her from head to foot, each time it came, faint and far-off as it was.

Her heart leaped with thankfulness when she came suddenly against the low stone wall of the cottage garden. She felt along it for the gate, and entered.

But no welcoming light shone from the windows, and her knocks remained unanswered. It was evident that no one was at home. After repeated attempts to make herself heard she made her way to the gate. The fog had lifted a little, and it was easy to follow the downward track towards the Manor House. Her footsteps quickened to a run as she left the cottage behind her. Though she could no longer hear that faint moaning cry, it still seemed to echo in her ears.

CHAPTER 11

THE SLIDING PANEL

When Marjorie reached the shrubbery path she was thankful to hear footsteps coming towards her. It was Mrs. Richards, whom Mrs. Bulteel had sent to look for her.

"Them fogs come on so sudden that it's aisy to get lost, my dear," she said as she turned. with Marjorie towards the house. " Mrs. Bulteel was in a rare fright when the doctor came in just now an' said how thick 'twas. But I knawed 'ee wasn't a maid to be afeard, my dear. An' so I told her."

"Oh, but I was frightened," Marjorie said with a shiver. "It wasn't the fog; it was that strange eerie cry from the Point. No wonder people don't like to cross the Point at night."

Mrs. Richards gave her a quick look. "Did 'ee

hear it, my dear? Now don't 'ee go an' tell Mrs. Bulteel so. Her's worrited enough as 'tis. An' St. Mawan folk do say Black Jasper allus knaws when trouble's to hand."

Marjorie might have tried to explain to the old woman that the cry, strange and fear-compelling as it was, was wholly due to natural causes. But Mrs. Richards went on, shaking her head with solemn foreboding.

"Now don't 'ee tell Mrs. Bulteel, my dear. Mr. Bulteel's took worse. The doctor's fair anxious about 'en. An' if her was to knaw Black Jasper's walkin' tonight—"

Marjorie interrupted her. "Oh, is Mr. Bulteel worse? He seemed so much better this afternoon."

"'Twas hearin' about the bank, my dear. He guessed summat was wrong from Mrs. Bulteel's face when she come in with her ladyship. And he got it out of 'em somehow. I s'pose they thought 'twas best to tell 'en. He seemed to bear it wonderful at first, an' began to talk o' goin' down to the bank first thing tomorrer mornin', to show hisself behind the counter. But jist as the words was in his mouth the poor dear went off in a fit, an' he'd only jist come round when Mrs. Bulteel sent me off to look for you."

Greatly distressed, Marjorie hurried on to the

house. As she entered the hall Mrs. Bulteel came out of the dining-room, and Marjorie caught a glimpse of Lady Barmouth and the doctor standing by the window, deep in anxious talk.

Mrs. Bulteel came quickly towards her with an exclamation of relief. "My child, I was frightened about you. The fog came on so suddenly. But you did not lose your way?"

"Not a bit of it. I got quite easily to the cottage. I could make no one hear, though; they must all be in the town still. But how is Mr. Bulteel?"

Marjorie asked it very anxiously, holding Mrs. Bulteel's hands tight. Mrs. Bulteel looked up at her, her lips quivering. "He is asleep. He will sleep for hours, Dr. Bell says. And if his mind can be kept at rest he will soon be well. But I am frightened of tomorrow, Marjorie. How are we to keep the truth from him? And it will break his heart if—"

But Marjorie would not let her go on. She tried to comfort her by talking of the help her cousin Robert was to bring from Plymouth, and after a little while something almost like a smile came to Mrs. Bulteel's pale lips.

Neither Mr. Prior nor Lady Barmouth had told her how great the chances were against Robert Carew being successful in the object of his long night-journey, and she found it easy to hope. And young as Marjorie was, there was help and comfort in her very presence. She eagerly caught at Marjorie's suggestion that she should spend the night at the Manor House instead of going back to Kitty at the Vicarage. Mr. Bulteel was in the big state bedroom over the dining-room, she told Marjorie, and she and Mrs. Richards meant to sit up with him all night. She would not let Marjorie sit up, but there was a bed in the dressing-room close by, and it would be a comfort to her if Marjorie slept there.

The night passed quietly. Marjorie lay awake for an hour or two after lying down, and once she stole to the bedroom door to ask Mrs. Bulteel if there was anything she could do. But she fell asleep at last, and did not wake till the gray dawn was breaking.

She heard Mrs. Richards leave the bedroom and go downstairs, and she hurriedly dressed and followed her. She found her in the great raftered kitchen stirring the smouldering turfs on the hearth into a blaze. She scolded Marjorie for getting up so early, but it was plain that she was glad of her company. Mrs. Bulteel had slept for an hour or two, she told Marjorie, and Mr. Bulteel had not stirred a finger all night.

"He's slep as peaceful as a newborn babby, my dear. 'Twas that stuff the doctor gave 'en. Hull be glad o' a dish o' tay as soon as the kettle boils. An' I've got a few broth here warmin' for my maister. He's out most nights at lambin'-time. Would 'ee be afeard to stop down here while I take the tay up, Miss Marjorie, an' unbolt the door to 'en when he comes. With highway robbers about us, honest folk have got to bolt the doors, though many a night I've gone to bed and left it on the latch."

Truth to tell, Marjorie would far rather have taken up the tea to Mrs. Bulteel than remained in the great kitchen, where the shadows only seemed the darker for the light of the solitary candle. But she put a bold face on it, and Mrs. Richards never guessed how her heart beat as she lighted her through the panelled passage, and then stood at the bottom of the broad shallow stairs till the old woman had reached the upper landing, where the daylight shone redly in through an eastern window.

Carrying the candle carefully in her hand, she set out on her return journey to the kitchen. The kitchen door was open, and there was something friendly in the warm glow that streamed from the hearth. She went quickly towards it, but just as she reached the threshold of the door, she stopped. Her eye had fallen on one of the granite blocks of the pavement close to the panelling on the right hand of the threshold. It bore traces of having once been roughly carved, and Marjorie, forgetting her fears in her curiosity as she remembered what the vicar had told her about the three-dragon stone in the passage, knelt down to examine it. Yes, there was the head of one of the dragons, and something that looked like the tail of another, and again something that was like either the head or tail of a third, just as you chose to regard it. And above it, though a little to the left, was the date 1607.

Marjorie had placed her candle on the floor to examine the defaced stone, and its light fell strongly on the dark corner of the panelling by the great granite block that formed the threshold. Even here the oak was carved; close to the threshold stone there was one of the heavy knobs or bosses that were found at intervals round the bottom of the panelling. As Marjorie thought of the figures in her Milton, she felt a sudden, thrilling conviction that here in this spot was to be found the clue to their meaning. Trembling with sudden excitement, she began to search for the cross; the next moment a little cry broke from her lips. She had found it! The light was shining full on the bossy knob, and there, almost hidden by the curled-up rim of the ornament, a tiny cross was cut.

With fingers that shook a little she pressed it,

feeling a dull sense of disappointment when no result followed. But she would not give up, she pressed again with all her strength. And there came a sudden click ; the whole heavy panel began to move, to slide into the wall, and Marjorie found herself looking into a narrow stone passage whose walls and floors were dark and damp with age.

It was only a hasty look she gave; then she quickly pushed the panel back into its place and hurried into the kitchen. She was thankful to hear Mr. Richards' heavy step outside. The sight of that dark mysterious passage had filled her with cold terrors.

Richards was a stolid, unimaginative man, the most un-Cornish of Cornishmen. But the news of Marjorie's discovery had a remarkable effect on him. He dropped his pipe on the stone floor, where it lay disregarded in a score of pieces, while he stared incredulously at her, a dull flush of excitement rising in his honest face.

"You'm jokin', miss," he gasped. "It aint true, be it?"

To convince him Marjorie took him outside the kitchen and showed him how the spring worked. She felt brave with this big strong man at her side, and proposed that they should explore a little. But Richards drew back in unaffected alarm. "I'll wait a bit, miss. Vicar ought to know. I'll go down an' tell 'en. He always belayed there was a secret passage hereabouts."

But the vicar was too anxious about the fortunes of the bank to be able to spare time to explore the mysterious passage that morning, and if it had not been for Mrs. Richards its secret would have been left undiscovered till later in the day.

She had been as excited as her husband about the sliding panel, and being endowed with a livelier curiosity and a pluckier spirit she could not rest till she found out where the secret passage led.

Kitty came from the Vicarage directly after breakfast. Mrs. Bulteel ran down to speak to her for a moment, and then hurried back to her husband, who was slowly beginning to recover consciousness after his long night's sleep.

Kitty was deeply distressed at her aunt's worn looks. "Oh, Marjorie, how dreadful it all is!" she said. "Do you know that there have been crowds of people going into St Mawan ever since daybreak this morning. I could hear wheels continually passing my window. Mrs. Fortescue says the bank must stop payment today. Even if Mr. Carew was to bring as much as a thousand pounds in gold from Plymouth it would do no good.

And she does not believe he can get that. The Plymouth banks will be afraid of a run on them. It is dreadful for Uncle James." And Kitty's eyes filled with real, unaffected tears.

Marjorie gave her a warm hug. "After all," she was saying to herself, "you cannot tell what people are really like unless you go through some trouble with them." But aloud she said cheerfully: "I am going to believe that cousin Robert will bring money enough, Kitty. I wonder how soon he will be here. Not yet—it is not nine o'clock. How slowly the clock ticks this morning! Do you think he is at Bodmin yet?"

While Marjorie was speaking, Mrs. Richards came into the hall from the kitchen, holding a candlestick in each hand. There was a determined expression on her small, clearly-featured face.

"Miss Marjorie, I be goin' down that there passage. Will 'ee come along weth me? I ain't goin' to wait for Richards nor vicar nor nobody. Here's a candle for 'ee, and I've got the tinder-box in my pocket. Come along, do 'ee, my dear. There's that inside me I can't fight against no more; I've got to go. Be 'ee afeard to come?"

A little bit of Marjorie was afraid, but she scorned to acknowledge that part of herself. She seized the candle, and laughing at Kitty's entreaties, she followed Mrs. Richards.

Kitty would go no farther than the entrance to the passage, but she promised to wait there till they returned. She sat down on the kitchen step, straining her ears to catch the sound of their retreating footsteps, and fancying every moment that she was about to hear a blood-curdling shriek. But the footsteps died away, and dead silence followed for some moments. Then came the sound of flying steps—Marjorie running back, fast, along the passage.

Kitty started to her feet, feeling sure something dreadful had happened to make Marjorie run like that. But her first glance at Marjorie's face banished her fears. It was radiant.

"Kitty, come, do come! It is wonderful! Give me your hand; it is only a few steps. No, I am not going to tell you. I want you to see for yourself."

Kitty yielded. The look on Marjorie's face would have made her follow her anywhere. And, as Marjorie said, she had not far to go. A few yards along a narrow, unevenly-paved passage, then a sudden turn and a descent of a few steps, then another length of narrow pass-age, and she found herself in a small chamber, or cave, cut out of the solid rock.

The Mystery Of An Old Murder

Kitty went no farther than the door. She stopped there, spell-bound, for the place seemed full of gold! The stone table in the middle was literally covered with it—heaped up with guineas, as if someone had been pouring them out upon it from the empty brandy kegs standing by. And there were other brandy kegs against the wall still full of golden coins, while a canvas bag at Mrs. Richards' feet had been half-emptied of its contents, which lay in glorious splendour on the ground about it.

"Where did it all come from?" gasped Kitty at length, when she could find her voice. "Whose is it, Marjorie?"

Marjorie was half-crying, half-laughing in her excitement. "It is cousin Robert's, Mrs. Richards says. His grandfather must have hid it here."

"An' his great-grandfeyther, my dear, an' his feyther afore 'en," said Mrs. Richards solemnly. "It must ha' took a hunderd year an' more to save all this." She bent down and picked up the canvas bag she had begun to empty on the ground. "We'll carry this back along weth us, Miss Marjorie. Seein' is be-lavin', as they say."

Marjorie put her hand out to stop her. "Don't you think we had better leave it all as it is for cousin

Robert to see, Mrs. Richards. I cannot understand about that bag. It does not look as if it had been here long. And look,"—she took up the top of one of the little kegs as she spoke,—"this wood has been split quite lately. Could somebody have got here through the caves, Mrs. Richards, do you think?"

Kitty gave a faint shriek. "Oh, Marjorie, those footsteps we saw! Come away. Don't stay here; it isn't safe."

Mrs. Richards had dropped the bag, staring in a startled fashion at Marjorie. "I do belave you'm right, my dear. Us be jist in time. Don't 'ee be so afeard, Miss Kitty. My master'll be back by now, run an' bring 'en in, my dear. I'll stay here an' look arter the money. Go back weth her, Miss Marjorie, the poor maid's jist frightened to death."

Kitty was thankful to get back to the daylight, but she would not let go of Marjorie's hand even then. And they hurried out together to find Richards.

"And then we must go to meet cousin Robert," cried Marjorie, with sparkling eyes, "for the bank will be all right now, Kitty. There must be thousands of pounds there, Mrs. Richards says,—and all in golden guineas!"

CHAPTER 12

THE RUN ON THE BANK

As Kitty said, people had begun to pour into the town before the sun was up. At nine o'clock there was scarcely standing-room in the High Street, and those who had fought for and gained places close to the bank doors had hard work to prevent themselves being pushed away by the surging, swaying crowd.

Fear is the most selfish of the emotions, and neighbourly feeling, so strong among Cornish folk, was almost forgotten that morning. Not quite, however.

The vicar, looking down from the drawing-room window with eyes that had pity in them, as well as anxiety, on the faces of those below, changed almost out of recognition by the fear that sharpened every feature, saw old Auntie Polwhele being pushed through the crowd by kindly force, those in front making room for her to pass, and those behind thrusting her gently forwards, till the poor trembling old soul was close to the bank doors, her little bundle of notes safely in her hand. An odd, quavering, half-ashamed cheer went up from the crowd when they saw her on the steps.

"You'm safe now, Aunt Martha! You'm all right!" they called to her, and then clutched their own notes tighter, each trying to edge a step nearer the pavement and thrust his neighbours back.

The vicar turned away with a choking sensation in his throat. Deeply anxious as he was for the Bulteels, he had only pity for that panic-stricken crowd.

He went downstairs to the back parlour, where a group of the banker's friends had gathered to assist the old head-clerk with their advice. They sat, pale and anxious, round the table. Ten o'clock was drawing near, and there was no sign of Robert Carew.

"I knew he could never do it. I told him it was impossible," said Mr. Hargreaves, the largest land-owner in the parish, except Robert Carew. "Just think of the state of the roads, Fortescue. He cannot be here."

"He will be," said the vicar confidently. "It is not ten o'clock yet, remember."

"Very nearly," murmured Mr. Pengelly, the

Wesleyan grocer, glancing at the clock on the mantelpiece. How the hands were galloping! He had a large balance in the bank, and the cold grasp of fear had laid hold of him. But he meant to be loyal to Mr. Bulteel, who had helped him over a rough bit of road a year or two before.

It was now within a minute or two of ten. Fists began to beat on the closed doors; a dull, inarticulate, terrifying sound, the voice of a threatening crowd, swelled louder and louder.

Mr. Prior, his knees visibly trembling under him, looked from one white face to another. " Gentlemen, what am I to do?" he asked.

In the dead silence that followed his despairing question, the timepiece began to strike, its silvery chime being followed an instant after by the deeper notes of the church clock. The old clerk wrung his hands, and the tears burst from his eyes. He appealed to those around him again, in a voice that was like a cry :

"Gentlemen, what am I to do?"

The question had not left his lips, no one had had time to answer it, when the hammering at the doors suddenly ceased. For an instant there was silence outside the bank, as well as in; then came the sound of shouting from the bottom of the street, a loud unmistakable cheer! Mr. Hargreaves sprang to his feet. "Prior, open the doors! Carew has come! Be quick! Don't let them say Bulteel's kept them waiting for a moment!"

The old white-headed clerk himself rushed out, and drew back the heavy bolts and flung wide the doors just as the last notes of the church clock died away. He had been waiting in sickening dread for that moment ever since the bank closed the night before. But how different the reality was to his visions of it! The crowd, indeed, flowed in as the doors opened, pressed forward by the weight of those behind. But there was no rush to the counter, no frenzied demands for the gold he could not give. A few over-cautious women, Aunt Polwhele among them, exchanged their notes for gold, but the rest of the crowd had lost all their fears. They were cheering like mad people, throwing hats and caps and handkerchiefs into the air to welcome the trap that was coming up the street with Robert Carew and the young clerk sitting in front, and the back heaped up with brandy kegs that literally overflowed with gold.

From lip to lip the news had gone like a lightning flash. Robert Carew had found his grandfather's hoards, thousands on thousands of golden guineas, and was bringing them to the bank to pay them into his account. And the panic was over. Bulteel's was safe!

· · · · · · ·

An hour afterwards Robert Carew was sitting alone in the dining-room. Breakfast had been prepared for him, but he had pushed it away untasted; and he was now sitting with his head supported by one hand, staring out into the garden, his dark eyes full of painful thought. The vicar, before going to the Manor House to see how Mr. Bulteel bore the good news, had tried to make him promise to take some rest. But weary as he was—he had not slept for two nights, and had driven more than a hundred miles in the last eighteen hours — sleep was impossible. He had never felt so intensely wakeful in his life. Though for Mr. Bulteel's sake he had rejoiced in Marjorie's discovery, for the coin he had been able to collect in Plymouth at such short notice would have proved wholly insufficient for the needs of the bank; though his heart had throbbed with responsive gladness as he heard the cheers of the crowd, he had hated the sight of the gold itself. He believed that his father must have somehow learnt of the hidden treasure, and finding Mr. Vyvyan alone, had tried to force the secret from the helpless old man. A violent quarrel, a struggle, had ensued, and his father had fled from the house in the darkness, the guilt of murder on his soul.

For some time Robert Carew had clung to the hope that his father was innocent; that if, indeed, it was he who fired that fatal shot, it had been by accident, with no intent to kill. A thousand times over he had pictured to himself how it might have happened. His grandfather, wild with rage at the unlooked-for appearance of the man he hated, might have rushed upon him, old man as he was, and attacked him with the heavy stick that had been found beside him. To defend himself, his father had drawn the pistol, and in the struggle it went off, killing Mr. Vyvyan on the spot. He could not, would not believe, black as his father's flight had made things look against him, that he had deliberately been guilty of murder. And as for the other charge brought against him, that he had sold information to the French, he put that aside with scorn. His father had no need to be defended against such a lie as that!

But very soon he was forced to give up his belief in his father's innocence. He had made the acquaintance of a French prisoner, an officer on parole, and when in his company one day, was painfully startled to see him wearing a ring that had belonged to his grandfather, and which had the Vyvyan crest stamped on the inside. In answer to his inquiries, the officer readily told him its history. He had won it at cards from an Englishman who had had to fly his country for some reason, and was living at Paris in the service of the Government. It was not the only thing he had won from him, and he showed Robert another ring, an intaglio with a finely-cut head of Medusa. Robert knew every line in those snaky coils about her head. His father had constantly worn the ring.

He managed somehow to hide his profound emotion, and the French officer never guessed. it. But he saw he was interested in his renegade countryman, and told him all he knew about him. He had called himself Jean Carois, and passed for a Belgian; only a few knew that he was an Englishman. He bore a bad reputation, and at last, after being concerned in a brawl that ended in murder, he was sentenced to the galleys for a term of years, which had not yet expired.

Robert could feel no doubt that Jean Carois was his father John Carew, and the iron entered deep into his soul. From that moment he shrank from the society of his fellow-men, as one with a brand upon him. He felt he could never go back to the Manor House now, never disturb Nell by reminding her of his existence. The memory of that convict in the galleys never left him. It poisoned his life.

He had lived chiefly in London, employing himself in literary work, but writing always under a feigned name, and caring nothing for the reputation he began to make in the world of letters. Only urgent matters of business connected with his estate had brought him to Cornwall. He had never intended to enter the town at all, or allow his presence at the Manor House to be known more than was inevitable. And though he could not resist the temptation to look at Nell's home, he had been careful that only Tamsin should see him. He had come and gone in the darkness.

Circumstances had forced him to depart from his intention as far as St. Mawan was concerned. For two days he had taken a leading part among his townsmen, had felt and acted as though he was one of them, had been welcomed home with a heartiness that had deeply touched him. But now that the need for his help was over, and there was no more for him to do, he longed to get back to his solitary lodgings in London; if it had been possible he would have gone that very day.

His gloomy thoughts were broken in upon by Mr. Prior. The old clerk came hurriedly in. "Mr. Carew, would you step into the bank, sir. Tregelles is here with the strangest story. His money has been stolen. And he says that Captain O'Brien is missing. Captain O'Brien is his lodger. You saw him here yesterday, a gentleman with blue spectacles."

"Did I see him? I do not remember. He is Mrs. O'Brien's cousin, an Indian officer, is he not? But what has he to do with Tregelles's money? Tregelles does not accuse him of taking it, does he?"

"That is exactly what he does," said Mr. Prior, trying to repress a chuckle. It was evident that he found a spice of enjoyment in Tregelles's misfortunes. "But come in and speak to him, sir. He's just crazy. Old fool, why did he not leave his precious money with us! He deserves to lose it."

"He must be crazy to accuse Captain O'Brien," said Robert, rather impatiently. "But I will speak to him, Prior. You had better send for the constable."

It was plain that Tregelles had been driven very nearly out of his wits by the loss of his money. Robert found it difficult to make sense at first of his confused story, told as it was in disjointed, half-inarticulate sentences. When he spoke of Captain O'Brien, he could hardly get his words out. Fury seemed to choke him.

But he cooled down a little under Robert's incisive questioning, and at last was brought to admit that his only reasons for suspecting the captain were that his missus couldn't abide him, and that he had apparently disappeared from the neighbourhood.

"Dan Tregony met 'en goin' home yesterday afternoon jist afore four o'clock. Us was in the town then, my missus an' me. He had the house to hisself for four hours an' more. But there wasn't no sign of 'en when us got home. He'd gone, an' the money with 'en. I'm as sartain he took it, Maister Robert, as if I'd seed 'en with these eyes."

"But you did not miss the money till this morning, you say? Did you not feel anxious about your lodger when you found he did not come home last night?" Robert asked. " It is his custom to come home, I suppose?"

"Us thought he was out sarchin' for the highwayman. The night afore he never come home till daybreak. Maister Robert, you may belave me or disbelave me, but he's got my money. An' maybe he's got the diamonds too."

"Come, come, Tregelles, this won't do," exclaimed Robert. "I'm sorry for you, but anybody may have broken into your house if you left it empty. And Captain O'Brien is a stranger here. Why, he might have fallen over the cliffs. We must set to work to search for him."

The Mystery Of An Old Murder

Tregelles shook his head, his face settling into its most obstinate lines. But Robert's suggestion had a different effect on Mr. Prior and Mr. Pengelly, who had been called in to assist at the colloquy. They looked at each other with startled faces.

"The fog!" ejaculated Mr. Pengelly; and the old clerk addressed Robert in an anxious voice.

"There was the thickest fog I remember for years for an hour or two last night, Mr. Carew. It's as likely as possible he's met with an accident, when you come to think of it. He told me only yesterday how weak his eyesight was. Let us hope we shall not find the poor gentleman at the bottom of Blackdown Cliffs."

CHAPTER 13

A RESCUE

Kitty was in the most radiant mood that morning. She no longer had to complain of St. Mawan being a dull place; the last few days had been brim-full of excitement. And now everything had come right Mr. Bulteel was fast recovering, the danger to the bank was over, and Marjorie's discovery had made her cousin a rich man, so that people would now be glad to forget what his father had done.

Certainly the diamonds were missing still. But Cornwall was not like London; the thief was sure to be discovered, it was only a question of a day or two.

"How can you be so low-spirited, Marjorie?" she remonstrated. "What can be the matter? You ought to be as happy as possible after what you have done. For it is you who saved the bank, everybody is saying so."

"It was cousin Robert's money," said Marjorie

softly. "But I am glad I found it."

"Then look glad," demanded Kitty, drawing a little nearer her. They were sitting in the fir-wood, on the red trunk of a fallen tree. Marjorie had her lap full of primroses, which she had been picking in the little dell below. She was tying them up into loose bunches for the little blue Nanking bowls in the Vicarage drawing-room. But her fingers moved slowly, and her face was far too grave to please Miss Kitty.

"There was nothing in your letters, no bad news?" Kitty went on, bent on finding out what it could possibly be that was troubling her. "What long ones they were, Marjorie! But there was no bad news in them?"

Marjorie looked up with the smile that always came when she talked of home. "Of course not, Kitty. It was all good news. You must read Jack's letter when Mr. Bulteel has finished with it. He thinks that the war will end before long. What must it be like to have peace, Kitty! The first thing I can remember is father reading something from the newspaper, and mother and Aunt Nell looking very sad. We were going to war again, mother told me. And there has been war ever since."

But Kitty was not interested in the prospects of

peace. She wanted to find out what was troubling Marjorie. "Do tell me what made you sigh so just now, Marjorie. I shan't believe you are going to have me for a real friend if you do not tell me."

Marjorie looked quickly up, and Kitty saw there were tears in her eyes. "It is only that I was thinking of cousin Robert."

"And of Aunt Nell," she might have added. Primroses were her aunt's favourite flowers, and she knew why now. She had never seen lovelier primroses than these from the little dell below the Manor House.

"That money will not make him any happier, Kitty. He was only glad about it because of Mr. Bulteel. And but for that I could wish I had never opened that panel."

"Money is always a good thing," said Kitty sagely. "Whatever makes you say you wish you had not found it?"

"I don't wish it; I am glad," said Marjorie hastily.

She could not explain to Kitty, but she instinctively knew how her cousin was feeling. He was glad too, and yet the discovery was intensely painful to him.

She had finished tying up the primroses, and she

put them in her basket and jumped up. "Let us go up to the cliff's, Kitty. The sea must be glorious this morning."

Kitty eagerly agreed. She had no love for the sea, but she was tired of sitting still.

She went back to the subject of the hidden treasure as they passed from the fir-wood out on the open down.

"Marjorie, do you really think that somebody had found out the way through the caves to that room? Did you show your cousin that bag?"

"No, I never thought of it again. There was so little time. Hark, Kitty! Did you not hear something? What was it?"

Kitty clutched her arm with a little shriek. "Marjorie, come back! It is that cry from the Point; it frightens me. Come back!"

Marjorie lifted her hand. She had turned paler than Kitty. "Hush!" she said. "Listen, Kitty."

Kitty dragged at her arm again. "It is; I can hear it quite plainly now. Oh, do come back, Marjorie!"

"But, Kitty, it is low tide. It cannot be that cry. Yet, listen! It is exactly as I heard it last night, only louder." She dragged her arm from Kitty's, and ran forward to the ridge of the downs. But it was only a moment she stopped there. She flew back. "Kitty, it comes from the mine; there is someone there. Someone has fallen into the shaft! Run back to the house quick, and get Richards to come with ropes. I saw some men ploughing in the field just now; I will go and call them."

• • • • • • • •

Robert was just starting for the harbour, to get a party of men together to search the cliffs, when one of the clerks came running after him to say that Richards had come to the house through the garden, and wanted to see him.

"They have found the captain, sir," he added. His voice came in gasps. The amazement with which he had listened to Richards' astounding story had almost taken away his breath. "He was in the mine-shaft, clinging to the timbers at the top. And he'd got the diamonds on him, Mr. Carew. He was the highwayman."

Robert learnt further details from Richards as

they walked back to the Manor House together. Mr. Bulteel had sent an urgent message, begging him to come home at once, as he wished most particularly to see him. Captain O'Brien had been carried to Tregelles's cottage. Dr. Bell was with him. They had sent for the doctor as soon as they got him out. He was quite conscious, but the shock and exposure had been too much for him. In Richards' opinion he was a dying man.

"How 'twas he lived through the night passes me," Richards said in a voice that had very little pity in it. "Thieves has got nine lives, like cats, I reckon. He must be a wily one,—eh, Maister Robert? He's desaived every mother's son of us; for he ain't Cap'n O'Brien more than I be. An' if it hadn't been for the fog, he'd have been off weth them diamonds, and Tregelles's guineas into the bargain. A mighty good thing that shaft's niver been filled up, sir."

"We'll have it filled up now," said Robert, with a shudder. It was horrible to think of the poor wretch clinging, all the long night through, to the rotting beam, shrieking in vain for help.

"Where do you think he was going, Richards? Could he have meant to walk to Bodmin? He must have known he would be missed. And he could not have carried that money. Those bags must be heavy."

"Heavy enough," said Richards, with a chuckle. " They'm lying at the bottom o' the mine-shaft now, sir. The money would be better in the bank, wouldn't it? 'Twill cost Tregelles a pretty penny to get it up, I'm thinkin'. He dropped the bags, you see, to save hisself. 'Twas a marvel he didn't go to the bottom too. He couldn't have held on much longer, he told us. The timbers he'd got his feet on was givin' away. A moment or two more an' he'd have gone down like a stone, an' us shouldn't have seen no more of 'en."

By this time they were close to the house, and Richards went off towards the stables, while Robert crossed the lawn to the hall door. Mrs. Bulteel was waiting alone in the hall, and she came quickly to meet him, smiling, but with tears in her eyes. Robert took her outstretched hands and pressed them gently, himself much moved.

"Shall I go up to Mr. Bulteel?" he asked.

"In a moment. I want to thank you, Robert, but I can't. But for you—"

"It is Marjorie we must thank," he said lightly. "Where is she?"

"She has gone to the cottage with some broth for that poor creature in the shaft. Poor Kitty was much too frightened to go with her. She is lying down, quite knocked up. It was Kitty and Marjorie who heard his cries—did you know that, Robert? What an awful, awful night it must have been for him. I cannot but pity him, though he plotted so wickedly against us. He had the diamonds on him, Robert. He must have had them when he came into the Vicarage."

She shivered and cast a hasty look behind her, as if afraid even now he might suddenly appear. Her nerves had been thoroughly shaken by the events of the morning. She sobbed a little as she spoke.

Robert had not much more pity than Richards to spare for the discovered thief. He began to speak of Mr. Bulteel. "I suppose you have told him we had the diamonds safe. How is he, Mrs. Bulteel? Is it right for him to see me, do you think? I will not stay more than a moment."

"I do not think he will rest till he has seen you. He begged that Richards should go for you at once. Yes, he knows how the diamonds were found. Dr. Bell was here; they came to fetch him. And he said James should be told. I wish now that I had waited, it excited him terribly. But he will be more content when he has seen you, Robert. Will you go up? He wishes to see you alone."

Mr. Bulteel was sitting up in bed, propped up by

pillows. His ruddy complexion had faded to a dull blotchy white, and his skin hung in loose, flabby wrinkles round his eyes, making him look like an old man. Robert was shocked at his appearance. But he spoke cheerfully.

"I am only allowed to stay a moment," he said. "What you have to do now is to get well, Mr. Bulteel. There is no need to be anxious about anything. Prior is a host in himself at the bank."

Mr. Bulteel did not seem to hear what he was saying, though his eyes were fixed on his face. "Sit down, Robert," he said in a hollow voice. "There is something I must say to you, something you ought to know. God grant I am wrong, my boy."

Mrs. Bulteel waited in the hall with some impatience for Robert's reappearance. She felt that her husband was not strong enough for a lengthened interview, and even that day she found it in her heart to blame Robert, when the moments dragged themselves out and he did not come.

She heard him descending the stairs at last. He was walking very slowly. Her heart began to beat wildly again as she heard that slow, heavy step. What was he coming to tell her? She went to the foot of the stairs to meet him, and at the first sight of her face he spoke quickly. "I do not think our talk has done him harm, Mrs. Bulteel. Will you go to him?"

She caught his arm. "Robert, what is it? What has he told you? Is it anything Dr. Bell has said to him?"

He put his hand over hers. "No, no; he speaks hopefully of himself. Do not be alarmed." He paused a moment as if trying to find the right words, and then said quite simply, "He believes that this man who called himself Captain O'Brien is my father."

She fell back from him with a little cry of horror. "Oh, no, no, Robert, it cannot be!"

"I think it is very probable," he said, again taking refuge in the barest words. "I am going to the cottage to satisfy myself."

She let him go. Words failed her altogether before the agony she saw stamped on his pale, rigid face.

He crossed the hall, walking slowly but firmly, and she heard the door close behind him.

CHAPTER 14

CONCLUSION

The nearest way to the cottage was through the shrubbery and across the fir-wood. The path through the shrubbery was narrow and winding, and hemmed in on each side by thickly massed evergreens. To pass from this to the wood where the sunlight fell in golden shafts athwart the tall red trunks, and the wind was making solemn music in the swinging branches overhead, was like entering another world. The stony calmness with which Robert Carew had set out on his dreadful mission broke down as the beauty of the familiar place stole upon his senses. His breast heaved, a great sob broke from him. He stopped. Close by him there was the fallen tree-trunk on which Marjorie and Kitty had sat that morning. He sat down there. There were primroses, one or two, on the ground, which Marjorie had dropped. He picked one up and twisted it to pieces in his fingers, unconscious of what he was doing. He had no doubt that the dying man at the cottage was his father. Mr. Bulteel had said he could not be sure—he hoped he was mistaken. But Robert had no hope. Mr. Bulteel had never heard the story of Jean Carois.

How long he sat there Robert did not know. Such moments cannot be counted. He was roused by the sound of a step, hardly audible on the thick carpet of fir-needles which covered the path. He looked up, and saw the vicar coming towards him. He got to his feet. If it had been possible he would have avoided him, but he was already quite close. And when he saw Robert look up he quickened his steps. But he came close to him before he spoke. There were tears in his kind eyes. His voice was broken.

"Robert, I was coming to you," he said. "I—"

Robert's face had turned ashy white. The moment he had seen the vicar's face be had divined that he had something to say to him. He was coming from Tregelles's cottage. How could Robert doubt what his message was? But he could not bear to hear. He lifted his hand.

"I know," he said in a harsh voice. And then as he met the vicar's eyes he fell back a step, lifting his hand to his forehead. "No," he said, "I do not know.

What have you to tell me?"

For he saw that it was joy for him, not grief, which had filled those kind eyes with tears. And the strong man began to tremble like a child.

The vicar spoke very slowly, waiting a moment between each sentence. He wished the light to break gradually on Robert.

"I have just come from Tregelles's cottage. Robert, that man, Captain O'Brien as he called himself, is dying. He has made a confession. You will know who he is when I tell you his real name. It is Baroni. He knew you in Plymouth, he says."

He paused, waiting for Robert to speak, but Robert could not. He hardly breathed. His eyes were fixed on the vicar's face. He saw he had more to tell him. Mr. Fortescue went slowly on :

"He met Captain O'Brien at Lisbon, ill and friendless at a hotel. He died, and this man. Baroni, who had been condemned to the galleys in France, and had only lately made his escape, took his name. He had found out about that money Marjorie discovered this morning, Robert. He came to get it. But he had tried to get it once before. Do you remember that ship you and Nell saw off Blackdown Point. He was on board of her. He landed under the Point. It was he—he—"He broke off and began again, laying his hand on Robert's shoulder. "Robert, it was this man who came back to the inn for your father's horse; who sold his papers to the French. Can you understand? Your father never left the Manor House."

Robert stared at him. No, he could not understand, his brain was reeling. And the vicar went on in a solemn voice: "He came too late to defend your grandfather, Robert. He found him lying dead, shot by that villain. But he gave up his life rather than take the bribes Baroni offered him. Do you understand now, my dear boy? For fourteen years your father has been at rest, his body hidden in the caves. Baroni has confessed everything. Marjorie must have touched his wicked heart in some strange way, and he sent her for me. Sit down here, on this tree. Let me tell you all."

It was a strange story the vicar had to tell. Baroni had heard Mr. Carew speak laughingly of the treasure supposed to be hidden in the secret passage between the Manor House and Blackdown caves, and his visit to St. Mawan had been for the purpose of discovering this passage. He hid himself in the caves when he was supposed to be exploring the coast, and at last made his way to the small chamber in which Marjorie had found the gold. No gold was to be seen then, only a row or two of wooden kegs against the wall. But he watched till he saw Mr. Vyvyan enter on one of his stealthy night visits, and by following him he learnt the secret of the panel door. He had been largely engaged in secret traffic with France, not merely smuggling, but the selling of valuable information, and it was easy for him to get a ship with a captain and crew who would accept any explanation he chose to give about the contents of the brandy kegs. He came from Plymouth in this ship, escaping by a few hours from sudden arrest, and landed from a boat at the mouth of the cave. Leaving the boat to wait for him he made his way to the secret chamber. He might have made off with his booty and left no trace behind, had not Mr. Vyvyan, taking advantage of his servants' absence, come to visit his beloved hoards, and surprised him. The old man was unarmed except for his stick, and Baroni had his pistol. He rushed back into the house and shut the panel, intending to call for help. But Baroni had followed him, and pushed the panel back almost as soon as he shut it. Before he could reach the door leading into the hall, he fell, shot through the heart.

After listening for some moments to satisfy himself that the squire had been alone in the house, Baroni coolly rifled the body of his victim, taking among other things the snuff-box, whose lid he dropped afterwards in the cave on his way to the boats. He then went into the hall, intending to look through the rooms for any objects of value that might be portable. He was in the middle of the hall when he heard a step outside, and an instant after the great doorbell went echoing through the house. Before he could move or make up his mind what to do, the door was pushed open and Mr. Carew stepped into the hall, having determined beforehand not to wait for his ring to be answered, lest he should be turned back from the door.

His surprise on seeing Baroni was extreme. Baroni, however, was ready with an explanation which satisfied him for the moment.

Being in the town he had called on Mr. Vyvyan, he said, and finding him out had been loth to go without looking round the beautiful old hall. They walked round the hail together, and Baroni learnt that Mr. Carew had ridden from Padstow that morning, and put his horse up at the inn, and that the horse was to be sent to the Manor House to him if the squire proved to be hospitable enough to ask him to supper and he did not return before dusk. But though Mr. Carew talked freely enough he watched his friend with growing distrust, and Baroni's ill-concealed alarm when the suggestion was made that they should go into the kitchen to find out if the house was really empty, made him certain that he had something to conceal. To satisfy himself Mr. Carew insisted on entering the panelled passage, and Baroni led the way. But he flung the heavy door in Mr. Carew's face and made a dart for the secret panel. When he tried to shut it, however, it resisted his efforts, and he was still struggling with it when Mr. Carew, after one horror-stricken look at his father-in-law's body, rushed upon him. Baroni left the panel open and got back to the treasure chamber, hoping to be able to buy the silence of Robert's father, whose desperate need for money he was fully aware of. But he soon found that he had mistaken the character of the man he had to deal with. Mr. Carew wasted no words. He suddenly closed with him and wrested the pistol from his grasp. But Baroni had a knife hidden, and he used it with deadly effect. Mr. Carew staggered back, the life-blood spurting from a wound in his side. He never spoke again.

Half an hour afterwards Baroni got back to the boat. He told the men that he had changed his plans about the kegs, as he had to pay a visit to Padstow. They were to be waiting for him soon after midnight at a lonely spot on the coast near Padstow, which both he and the captain knew well. He had already formed the plan he afterwards carried out. He knew that even if the servants did not return till late, the boy from the inn would come with the horse and raise an alarm. It was necessary to leave the kegs till another time, and to divert suspicion from himself he determined to throw it on Robert's father. He was just his height and build, and with eyes and hair only a trifle darker. Dressed in the dead man's riding-coat and beaver, he completely deceived the servants at the inn. He reached Padstow and was on board the ship before the old servants got back to the Manor House. And by daybreak he was out of sight of land, on his way to a point on the French coast, where the captain knew a brig was waiting for him, with a cargo of brandy and tobacco on board. Baroni embarked on the French brig, as he had often done before. He was continually passing between France and England in his work as a spy. The English ship having taken on board the smuggled brandy and tobacco sailed for Plymouth. But it never reached port. A great storm arose that night and it was wrecked off the Lizard, every man on board being lost.

Baroni made his way to Paris, fully intending to return to St. Mawan to reap the reward of his double crime as soon as possible. But, as he grimly told the vicar, circumstances had rendered his return impossible till lately; a remark Robert could interpret better than the vicar, from his knowledge of Jean Carois' history. For it was now plain who Jean Carois was.

What the vicar told Robert Carew that morning was but the barest skeleton of the narrative here set forth, only just enough to make him understand the truth. Robert listened in silence, looking down on the ground, his lips set close together. He did not speak when the vicar had finished, but turned and gripped his hand. The tears were dropping fast over his face.

The vicar got up. "I will go on to the house. You would like to be alone a little."

He sat suddenly down again, putting his arm round Robert's shoulders. He was as dear to him as a son. "If I could tell you what this is to me, what it will be to us all. To have you back again, to see you in your right place. But I know what you are thinking. Robert, he died a soldier's death, he died for honour's sake. All these years he has been quietly at rest."

Robert averted his face. "You know—where?" he said in a low voice.

"Yes, he told me."

Both men were silent for a moment, thinking of that secret tomb in the caves. Then the vicar tried to lead the son's thoughts gently away from it

"Yes, he seemed eager to tell all at last. Yet but for Marjorie he might have died silent. Hardened villain as he is, that dear child seems to have touched some chord of pity in him. He had refused to open his lips to

Dr. Bell, but when he heard her voice at the door he asked to see her. And she persuaded him to send for me. The man has been fitly punished, Robert. He was taking the diamonds and Tregelles's guineas to the cave when he missed his way and slipped on the edge of the shaft. He meant to carry it all off at leisure. Not one of us suspected him, though Marjorie had a sort of horror of him from the first, she tells me."

"I should like to see Marjorie," Robert said, looking up. "Where is she?"

"At the Vicarage. I sent her home. Will you go down to her presently, Robert? Let me tell Mrs. Bulteel. And all the town must know."

The old vicar could not keep the ring of joyous triumph out of his voice. To have Robert back again at the Manor House, his father's name cleared, was what he had never dared to hope for. He felt a dozen years younger as he walked quickly towards the house to carry the glad news to the Bulteels.

Half an hour afterwards, Marjorie and Kitty were in the Vicarage garden, when Mrs. Fortescue came out to tell Marjorie that her cousin was in the drawing-room waiting to see her. She let her go in alone. She had already spoken to Robert.

Kitty looked after her, her blue eyes full of loving

admiration. " I wonder what he will say to her, Mrs. Fortescue. For it is all Marjorie's doing, all of it. And I brought her here. If Uncle James and Aunt Mary had not fetched her from Plymouth they would not have gone to Saltleigh, and then Marjorie would not have come here. Oh, how I hated the idea of coming to Cornwall! but I am very glad I came. Mrs. Fortescue, do you think Mr. Carew will live here now?"

Mrs. Fortescue smiled at her over her spectacles. "Perhaps he will find it too dull after London, my dear."

Kitty coloured up, but found it possible to laugh at this bit of teasing. "I always thought people who lived in the country must find it so dull," she confessed. "It seemed very funny to me at first to find you were all sorry for me because I had to live in London. But of course Mr. Carew will like to live in his own house. But it is dreadful to think of Mr. Carew's body being hidden away in the caves all these years. Will they bury him properly now, Mrs. Fortescue?"

"Of course, my dear," said Mrs. Fortescue, getting hastily up. The light gossiping tone in which Kitty was talking jarred intolerably on her, though she knew the girl meant no harm. "Come and help me sow some seeds, Kitty. You can never be dull if you have a garden. There is always something to do in it."

The Mystery Of An Old Murder

Marjorie was glad to go to her cousin. There was something she wanted to say to him, something that she had not told Mr. Bulteel. For a moment or two she found it difficult to speak at all; she had begun to sob a little in sheer happiness of heart when she saw him. He was very pale and grave, but every line in his face seemed changed. And there was a light in his eyes no one had seen there for fourteen years.

He would not begin at once to talk of what was filling both their hearts. He talked of Mr. Bulteel and the bank, described to her the wonderful effect the sight of the gold had had on the waiting crowd; and then, when her tears were dried and he had made her smile at him, he spoke of Baroni's confession. She would not let him go on.

"Cousin Robert, it was not for me he did it. It was only because—because I reminded him of Aunt Nell. He told me that. She was the only person in the world who had ever made him wish to be a good man, he said. And it was for her sake he told the truth before he died."

Her mention of her aunt moved him deeply. Something in Marjorie's tone made him feel sure that she realized what it must be to him to hear Nell's name, and he understood Marjorie too well already to believe that she would have spoken thus unless she knew that

Nell loved him still. He had told himself that he need not fear, that their love for each other had not been the love "which alters when it alteration finds". But not till now had he been quite sure. It was as if Nell herself had spoken to him, bidding him put all fear away.

He stood for a moment looking at the dark line of firs on the distant hillside, which showed where the downs ended and the Manor woods began. Then he came back to Marjorie, who was sitting at the table wondering if it could be only two nights ago she and Kitty had sat there, looking over the portfolio of prints! And was it really only this morning that Mrs. Fortescue had asked her to pick some primroses for that little blue Nanking bowl! How all the world had changed since then!

Robert spoke abruptly. "Marjorie, I shall send Richards to Saltleigh with letters this afternoon. Should you like to go with him?"

Marjorie started up. It was what her whole soul had been longing for, but she had not dared to think possible.

"Oh, cousin Robert!" was all she could say.

He smiled at her. "We must find out what Mrs. Bulteel thinks about it. But you would be home before seven o'clock. And I should like you to tell them." He paused a moment, and then added impulsively, "Marjorie, shall you hate me very much if I try to take your Aunt Nell away from you?"

And if Marjorie found it difficult to speak, her look was answer enough.

THE END

ABOUT THE AUTHOR

Laura Brett was born and raised on both sides of the Atlantic Ocean. With an American dad, winters were spent in uptown New York, while the British ancestry of her mother secured wonderful summers in the English countryside.
Educated at Oxford and Stanford Universities, Laura spent most of her adult life travelling the world as a personal assistant to a well-known actor. During the long waits on film-sets Laura started writing short stories and poems, some of which were published to high acclaim. After writing several full-length novels Laura was confident enough to share one with the world. The Mystery Of An Old Murder is her first published novel.

33366454R00106

Made in the USA
Middletown, DE
10 July 2016